He slipped his arm around my waist and we walked that way awhile. My feet scarcely seemed to touch the ground. It seemed no time until we got to his house. "Here's my stop," he said.

As he turned to leave, I smiled. He smiled back and I felt faint with happiness. "Okay, then," he said, "see you tomorrow."

I floated the rest of the way home. I was so high that if I'd had an aerosol can of smoke, I could have written in the sky. I would have written, "Gabe loves me." That was certainly news that deserved to be written in the sky or spelled out in lights, or at the very least, embroidered on a T-shirt with hearts and flowers.

Dear Readers:

In our last letter we told you about *Journey's End*, the first of Becky Stuart's series featuring Kellogg, Carey and Kellogg's faithful dog, Theodore. In book #2, *Someone Else*, to be published in February, the famous trio solves another mystery: just where has Carey's neighbor gone? Theodore is the first to know, and you may be sure the answer is a surprise to all concerned.

Now we would like to call your attention to *Orinoco Adventure*, scheduled for January, Elaine Harper's first Romantic Adventure. Romantic Adventures are Blossom Valley Books that are not set in Blossom Valley. Each one will have a map so that you may follow for yourself the travels of the characters. Look for the words Romantic Adventure on the front cover, under the Blossom Valley arch. You'll be glad you did!

Nancy Jackson
Senior Editor
FIRST LOVE FROM SILHOUETTE

BLUE SKIES AND LOLLIPOPS
Janice Harrell

First Love from Silhouette

Published by Silhouette Books New York

America's Publisher of Contemporary Romance

SILHOUETTE BOOKS
300 E. 42nd St., New York, N.Y. 10017

Copyright © 1985 by Janice Harrell

Distributed by Pocket Books

ISBN: 0-373-06165-X

First Silhouette Books printing December 1985

10 9 8 7 6 5 4 3 2 1

America's Publisher of Contemporary Romance

Printed in the U.S.A.

RL 6.0, IL Age 11 and up

JANICE HARRELL is the eldest of five children and spent her high-school years in the small central-Florida town of Ocala. She earned her B.A. at Eckerd College and her M.A. and Ph.D. from the University of Florida. For a number of years she taught English at the college level. She now lives in Rocky Mount, North Carolina, with her husband and their young daughter.

Chapter One

When my true love, Mike Hollister, dropped me like a hot biscuit and took up with Mimsy MacRae, I took it hard. Very hard. And seeing him at school trotting after Mimsy like a loyal Pekingese, I felt even worse. In fact, by the end of a week of it, I found myself wondering if the French Foreign Legion took women.

Saturday morning I rolled out of bed with a groan, reminded myself that I'd gotten through a week of being without Mike and felt proud. Then I remembered that another week was just ahead and groaned again. I managed somehow to get on some clothes and stagger into the kitchen. Mom was there humming a little tune while she fried eggs. "Your SAT scores just came in the mail," she sang, flipping an egg over. "I hope you don't mind that I peeked at them."

I slumped into a chair. "Nope," I said.

"Don't you want to know what they were?" asked Mom.

I knew they must have been okay or Mom wouldn't have been singing. I remembered when my brother Blake's scores came in last year, Mom and Dad practically dressed in sackcloth and ashes. Mom said it was a mercy Blake had taken the test as a junior so that they had warning before it was too late. They took him right out of Millville Senior High and moved him to Westover Academy, where he could get personal attention. After that, Dad started taking his lunch to work in a bag, and we gave up the New York City vacation we had planned and went camping in the mountains instead because Westover Academy was not cheap. I supposed Mom was singing because she was glad such extreme measures were not going to be necessary in my case. Unlike Blake, I had always made good grades and I had the knack of doing well on standardized tests.

Mom laid the envelope on my plate. "Don't you think it would be better if your shoes matched?" she said, glancing at my feet.

I looked down and saw that I had somehow managed to put a penny loafer on my right foot and a tassel loafer on my left foot. Details. I had no time for details when my heart was breaking. "Later," I said. I pulled the scores out of the envelope and looked at them. I was surprised to see I had made a perfect score on the verbal section. That was nice.

You couldn't get any better than that. And as for the math section, considering I had been the only person in the examination room counting on my fingers, it wasn't a bit bad.

Mom slid an egg onto my plate, then pulled up a chair beside me. "Your father and I are so proud of you," she purred. "I expect it's quite unusual to make a perfect score on a section."

"Dad's already seen my scores?" I said.

"Oh, yes," Mom said. "I happened to be talking to Grandmother on the phone this morning and I mentioned them to her, too," she said.

Next we take out a full page ad in the paper, I thought. For a minute I wondered what Mimsy's scores looked like, then I reminded myself that if you had cute pouty lips and a giggle like hers you didn't need to be smart, and I winced.

"Are you okay?" asked Mom.

"Fine," I said bravely.

"Well, then eat that egg before it gets cold."

I looked at the egg sitting on a little slick of oil, its yellow yolk staring at me accusingly. "I guess I'm just not in the mood for eggs," I said.

Normally, this remark would have gotten me a little lecture on the valuable iron content of an egg, but today Mom whisked the egg away without a word and produced a fresh baked cinnamon roll. My stock was obviously high because of my SAT scores. I buttered the roll and bit into it. Luckily, I have never yet been so depressed I couldn't eat a cinnamon roll.

"Sweetheart," she said, sitting down beside me again, "I have the impression you're not really enjoying your junior year."

"I'm getting along all right," I said.

"You seem abstracted," Mom went on, "as if your mind's on something else."

"What makes you say that?" I said uneasily.

Mom glanced at the SAT report. "Well, for one thing, did you realize you had checked off on that form that you were an American Indian?"

Startled, I looked at the report. "My pencil must have slipped," I said.

"Your father and I have been talking about it," Mom said, "and we wonder if you wouldn't like more of a challenge at school."

What I would like would be roasting Mimsy MacRae over hot coals, but I had no intention of telling Mom that.

"Your father and I feel bad," she went on, "that Blake has gotten to go to Westover Academy when you have had to keep slugging away at Senior High where you don't get quite the individual attention you deserve."

"I like Senior High fine," I said. "Besides, we can't afford for me to go to the academy. It's killing us just to send Blake."

"True," said Mom, "but Grandmother has offered to foot the bill for your tuition."

I could see that while I had been sleeping the morning away things had been humming around me. Mom and Dad had read my SAT scores, talked to

Grandmother, and planned my future before I even got out of bed.

I swallowed hard. "She has?"

"That's right. Of course, Grandmother recognizes that Blake has special needs, but it's always bothered her that we sent him and not you."

"So you want me to go to the academy?" I said, not quite able to take it in. This had big implications.

"You could start right away, if you want," said Mom. "They're very flexible over there."

"I'm not sure I want to do that," I said. "I might miss my friends. And there's a chance I might get to play the piccolo in the band this year." At least, I added to myself, if one of the piccolos breaks his neck. I found myself thinking it would be heavenly not to have to watch Mike drooling after Mimsy anymore. The academy would be sort of like the French Foreign Legion, but without the sand flies and camels. I could live right here at home and still be almost in another world. And I wouldn't have to face Mike every day at school. The idea had a very strong appeal.

Just then I heard the whisper of Dad's wheels on the floor and turned. He had just come in the deck door from the garden, where to judge by the crumbs of dirt in his hair, he had been enthusiastically pulling weeds. "Have you told her?" he called cheerfully as he wheeled swiftly over to us.

My father was in a plane crash back when he was in the navy, before he met Mom, and he lost both legs. After they pulled him from the burning wreckage he spent a year in the hospital getting patched up, but nobody who knows my dad would be surprised to find out that he emerged from the disaster pretty much the same as ever. He had always been a good-looking guy and he still was. Furthermore, he was as optimistic and energetic as ever. The fact is that for a person like me, who was feeling more than a little downhearted, he could be pretty hard to take in the morning.

"How about those scores!" he crowed, ruffling my hair.

I managed a weak smile.

"So did Mom tell you what we want to do?" he said. "I talked to Stan Morrison, the headmaster at Westover, this morning and he said you could start Monday if you wanted to. So, what do you think?"

"I don't know," I said. "This is all so sudden." It seemed weird to me to be switching schools in November. And there was no denying it would be a big change for me. Millville Senior High was a big, disorderly public school with a first-rate band, a first-rate basketball team, and a real cross section of all sorts of kids. The academy was going to be different. It didn't even have a band or a basketball team, and I had the idea it was full of snooty rich kids in identical blazers.

"Stan told me they'd love to have a new flute in their chamber music ensemble," said Dad. "No more waiting in line for a chance to play a piccolo in the band. And in place of pep rallies, you'd be having art appreciation classes, visits to museums, trips to ballets, and concerts. Enrichment. Cultural opportunities.''

"I need to think it over," I said. But I didn't need to think it over long. How long could I stand seeing Mike turn on the water fountain while Mimsy pouted her pretty pink lips to drink from it? I needed a complete change of scene. To be specific, I needed a scene without Mike and Mimsy in it. "I'll do it," I said suddenly. Then I gulped. It was a big step.

After dinner that night I called my friend Stephanie and told her the news.

"You're kidding me!" she said. "You can't transfer just like that, right in the middle of the term."

"Dad says I can."

"You can't be serious," she said.

I thought of the way Mike had kissed the tip of Mimsy's nose Wednesday morning as he helped her down the steps of the bus. "I'm serious," I said grimly.

"Hold everything," she said. "I'm coming right over. We need to talk about this."

Stephanie picked me up fifteen minutes later, and we drove to the pizza parlor where we could talk. We holed up in a booth in the darkest corner.

"Are your parents making you do this?" she hissed.

"Nope," I said. "I need a change, Steph. I can't stand watching Mike with that girl one minute longer."

"He's only a boy," she said. "Just tell yourself it doesn't matter."

"It matters to me," I said.

"Why do you have to take it so hard?" she said. "Why can't you just roll with the punches?"

"I'm not the roll-with-the-punches type. I'm more the crumble-when-the-going-gets-tough type."

I had been thinking a lot about what must have caused Mike to drop me. I knew I had my father's looks—thick dark hair, wide blue eyes, and the kind of little smidgin of a nose that generations of Miss Americas have had. My looks were fine. And there was nothing wrong with my brain—look at those SAT scores.

"It's my personality he can't stand," I said glumly. "Once he got to know me really well he realized what a yucky person I am. I should have never let him get to know me. I should have just kept giggling, like Mimsy."

Steph sat there looking wise, like the guys who sell insurance on television. "I wish you'd get over the idea that it means anything that Mike...uh..."

"Dumped me?" I said.

"Started seeing Mimsy," she finished triumphantly. "Certain people just click. You know, it's bigger than both of them. They're made for each other—like Adam and Eve."

"Thanks, Steph," I said. "You're making me feel heaps better."

"It doesn't have anything to do with you that Mike's flipped over Mimsy. She's just his type." She lowered his voice. "Do your parents know that Mike is the reason you want to transfer?"

"Are you kidding? I know better than to tell my parents that."

"What you ought to do is rise above this Mike thing," said Stephanie. "Don't give up the ship. Turn your stumbling blocks into stepping-stones."

"Let a smile be your umbrella," I said. "Count your blessings instead of sheep. No, thanks, Steph. I get enough of that stuff at home. I'm going to just quietly slink away in defeat, if you don't mind."

Just then, Mike and Mimsy came in. Hand in hand, naturally. "I've got to get out of here," I said desperately to Stephanie.

"We haven't even ordered yet," she said. Then she looked up from the menu and saw Mike and Mimsy. "Uh-oh," she said. "Okay, Tish, steady now. Take a deep breath. We'll get you out of here."

I stood up, holding my chin high and charged out, Stephanie trailing along loyally behind me.

Unfortunately, my chin was up so high I wasn't watching exactly where I was going and, midway, I collided with a corner of the salad bar. The floor must have been slick, because the next thing I knew I was sitting flat on the floor amid some lettuce, cucumber slices, and radishes. A couple of pizza parlor employees in white hats came running. Worse, Mike and Mimsy came running. "Are you okay, Miss?" said one of the men in white hats, bending over me anxiously. "You didn't break anything, did you?" said Mike, kneeling beside me, his green eyes looking embarrassed and sympathetic. At least he didn't want me to break a leg, even if he didn't mind grinding my heart under his heel.

I pulled a sprig of parsley out of my hair. "I'm fine," I said. This is great, I thought. The first time Mike has noticed me since Mimsy came into his life, and I have to be sitting on the floor with parsley in my hair. I wished I was dead.

Stephanie helped me up and I limped my way toward the exit. At last we got outside into the darkness. I staggered toward Stephanie's car and slid in. I groaned. Stephanie got in the driver's seat and took out her keys. The neon sign that spelled PIZZA suddenly blinked on, shedding a red light on her curly hair and pug nose, so she looked like a jazzed-up cherub, but I was in no mood to appreciate fancy lighting effects. I felt terrible.

"Oh, dear," said Stephanie suddenly. "I think I left my coat inside."

I gave her a look.

"I'll get it tomorrow," she said hastily, and we drove off. I bent to wipe little drops of mayonnaise off my shoes with a handkerchief.

"My life is in ruins," I said bitterly. "Now Mike will always remember me the way he saw me last—sitting in a salad."

"Maybe transferring to the academy isn't such a bad idea after all," she said in a subdued voice.

Chapter Two

Monday morning I drove to Westover Academy with my brother Blake. Since, unlike public schools, the academy didn't have buses, Mom let Blake take her car most days.

"I guess I'm going to have to take you to school every day now," he said as we drove. "And give you a ride home, too." He looked martyred and heaved a heavy sigh.

There's only a year's difference between Blake and me, and until he got so tall, people were always asking if we were twins. But, actually, we aren't a bit alike. To sum it up in the briefest way possible—I am nice and he is not.

Unlike Blake, I have always tried my best to be a good kid. I write thank-you notes, listen to Mom's and Dad's advice, work hard at school, and do my best to keep my room neat. Blake is different. A person who wants to know his present to Blake has arrived had better send money and plan to let the canceled check serve as his receipt because Blake never writes thank-you notes. His room would be great for growing mushrooms commercially, and he hasn't worked hard in school since they gave up drawing crayon pictures of bunnies. As for listening to Mom's and Dad's advice, I've never seen anybody who could tune people out the way he can. When he doesn't want to hear what a person is saying, it's as if he lives on a different planet.

Mom and Dad say he has special needs. I say there's nothing wrong with him that a year in a high security prison wouldn't fix. Sometimes I think of that story in the Bible where Joseph's brothers get fed up with him and sell him to some passing camel traders, and I perfectly understand the motivation of those guys. But I guess I don't think I'd sell Blake if I had the chance. Not really. The truth is that I don't so much actually dislike him as I envy him. I envy him right down to my toes. I'd love to be like him and not give a flip about anything.

When we got to the academy, Blake pulled into the semicircular drive in front. "The headmaster's office is up front here," he said. "I guess you'd better check in there." He stopped to let me out, then sped off to the student parking lot without a backward glance. It didn't take much intuition to see that from now on he was going to pretend not to know me. I was on my own.

The minute I went into the school office, I knew I was in a new kind of place. The office at Senior High had always had a faint smell of old tennis shoes and mimeograph fluid and was jammed tight with kids getting hall passes. This office was not like that. It had a small, leafy tree in the corner. It had a carpet. And it was very quiet. The only sounds I could hear were the hum of an electric typewriter and the distant faint whir of the fan of the heating system. A student was in the office, but she didn't look like a real student. I mean, she didn't have bitten nails or a pimple on her face the way real people do. She looked too perfect. She was slender and her hair was so glossy it could have been vinyl. I found myself hoping she was not a representative sample of the student body.

I began to feel nervous. Possibly the quiet was getting to me, or possibly it was the way the shiny-haired girl was looking at me. I leaned on the counter a little for support. "Uh, I'm Tish Summerlin," I said to the secretary. "My father talked to Mr. Morrison this weekend and told him I'd be enrolling."

Just then Mr. Morrison stuck his head out of his office. "Send Tish right in, Mrs. Wright. I'll give her her schedule." He had a smooth, boyish face. I was beginning to feel as if I had fallen down the rabbit hole into Wonderland. The principal looked sweet, the students looked like models, and the office looked like somebody's living room. I didn't like it. At least when you stepped foot in Senior High you knew you were in a school.

The headmaster's desk was the size of a skating rink and was made of polished mahogany. He pulled open a drawer and got out a pamphlet. "Here's the student handbook," he said, handing it to me. "Look it over when you get the chance. We have a somewhat more strict dress code than Senior High, but I don't think you'll find that a problem. We encourage students to wear the school blazer, but it's not mandatory."

The school blazer was illustrated right there on the pamphlet's overleaf—one hundred percent wool with gold blazer buttons. Only two hundred and fifty dollars. It looked as if I'd be doing without the school blazer. I tried to remember whether Blake had a blazer or not, but I'd been so busy ignoring him lately that I couldn't be sure.

"We've signed you up for the same classes you had at Senior High," he said, handing me my schedule. "I hope you'll soon feel at home here." Then he smiled at me, showing dimples. Stepping out of his office, he called to the model girl who was standing by the potted tree pretending to read a mimeographed sheet but actually eavesdropping like mad. "Amelia," he said, "would you show Tish to her first class and help her find her way around?"

"Of course," said Amelia. "Follow me." As I followed her meekly out the office door I noticed she walked with a shuffle, like a model in a fashion show. Her hips somehow stayed absolutely still and all the action was from the knees down. I surreptitiously tried to see if I could do it, too, but we must have been made differently or something because I couldn't.

She glanced at my schedule. "You have Chemistry first," she said, "like me. After that I'll turn you over to Christie. She has Honors English and you can go there with her."

I cheered up some when I realized that the model girl wasn't in Honors English. She wasn't perfect after all. But so what if she wasn't smart, I reminded myself. She did have a school blazer. The gold buttons glittered as we turned to go into the classroom, and when she smiled at me her teeth were almost as glittery as the buttons. It was not, somehow, a friendly smile. "Here's home room," she said.

When we went in, Amelia introduced me to the teacher. "This is Tish Summerlin, Hr. Hardy," she said. "She's new." Then she flashed another of her cold forty-five karat smiles and slid into a desk on the front row. About twenty pairs of eyes were staring at me. I was sure I must be turning red. "Just find yourself a seat, Tish," Mr. Hardy said vaguely. "I believe there's one back there somewhere."

Back there somewhere was just where I wanted to be. As far back as possible. I edged along the wall straight to the last row and found an empty desk. But being in back did me no good. Everyone in the class turned around to look at me. I held myself together by counting how many people were wearing blazers. The answer was—a lot. It looked like a blazer factory in there.

"I believe that's just about all," Mr. Hardy was saying to the class. "Oh, by the way, people, did I remember to mention that the chamber music ensemble will be meeting Wednesday afternoons instead of Thursdays the rest of this term? Any ensemble members who have conflicts should notify Mrs. Wilson."

Suddenly I felt a warm breath on my hand. I jerked my hand back up to the desk and looked down, startled. The black, furry face of a Labrador retriever was staring up at me. A dog? I thought. Did they really let dogs come to class here?

I noticed, then, that the Lab was wearing a harness and that attached to it was a stout plastic handle more or less the shape of a squared-off trombone slide. When the guy in the desk ahead leaned over and scratched behind the dog's ears, I saw he was wearing dark glasses, and it suddenly hit me that he was blind. The Labrador retriever must be his Seeing Eye dog. I had never actually met a Seeing Eye dog. The boy with the dog was sturdy-looking with a thick neck like a bull and light brown hair that curled under just slightly. I noticed that like everyone else I had seen so far, he was wearing a blazer. By most people's standards, since he was blind, he would be considered to have bigger troubles than me, but on the other hand I could see that he was perfectly calm, whereas I was practically falling apart.

The bell for the end of home room rang, and the boy and his dog got up to go. Amelia appeared at my side. "Chemistry's next," she said. "Hi, Bryan."

He turned to look straight at her and smiled, "Hi, Amelia." I could tell this guy was very smooth. Not only did he recognize Amelia's voice, but it's got to take a lot of practice for someone who's blind to look straight at where a person's voice is coming from. He couldn't see Amelia, after all. Looking at her was a social ploy to make him seem more like sighted people. It worked, too. When he did it, it was hard to believe he couldn't see, which was the idea, I supposed.

"Bryan, this is Tish Summerlin," Amelia said. "She's new. But you're going to have to wait to get to know her because we've got to run off to Chemistry. Tish, this is Bryan Guthrie, who drives a Lincoln Continental. I know you want to be loved for yourself, Bry, but I couldn't resist."

"Hi," I said.

He flashed me a friendly smile, then Amelia and I sped off to Chemistry. Considering that Amelia walked like Huckleberry Hound, it was amazing the speed she could put on. I looked behind me to make sure Bryan wasn't nearby, then panted, "Goodness, he's blind! How did it happen?"

"I don't know," said Amelia coldly. "You don't go around asking people how they happen to be blind. They'd get pretty sick of it if you did."

I didn't see what was wrong with my asking. It wasn't as if I had asked Bryan directly. Curiosity is no crime. I felt as if Amelia were putting me in my place, and after that I didn't say anything else.

When we got to Chemistry class there was a bottleneck at the classroom door, and Amelia bumped into a tall boy with black eyebrows. He was the first person I had noticed who was not wearing a blazer. He wore old jeans and was in shirt-sleeves, which must have been chilly in the drafty halls.

"Hi, Gabe," said Amelia. She was sort of melting against the doorjamb as she looked up at him. She even shivered a little, as if an electric current were passing through the doorjamb. Whoever this guy was, he wasn't having any trouble holding Amelia's attention.

I edged past them into the classroom. It did not escape my notice that Amelia had not introduced me to Gabe. Still, I would probably get to meet him later.

I went over to the Chemistry teacher, Mr. Stokes, and introduced myself to him, then quickly slipped into a seat before the bell rang. I was hoping to be inconspicuous. I saw that the girl who sat down in front of me wasn't wearing a blazer, and I began to feel a little better. Maybe it was going to be possible, after all, to sustain life and maintain my self-esteem around here without a two-hundred-and-fifty-dollar blazer.

Gabe slid into a seat across from me just as the bell rang. "I hope you all are ready for our test," said Mr. Stokes. The whole class moaned as he began handing out mimeographed sheets, and for a second I felt panicky. Did he expect me to take the test? But when he got to me, he just handed me a chemistry book and said, "Why don't you familiarize yourself with the textbook, Tish, while we take the test. If you need any help catching up, I hold a tutorial Wednesday afternoons. I've turned down a page for you so you can see where we are.''

Dog-earing the page of a book had been a major offense at Senior High, but I guessed it didn't matter around here, where the book was going to end up on my parents' bill anyway. I just hoped Grandmother had figured in all these hidden expenses.

Mr. Stokes went on handing out the test, and I opened the book. It was the same one we had had at Senior High, so I already knew what it was like. But it turned out they were four chapters ahead of where we had been in my old class. Chemistry was not my best subject, so it looked as if I might be attending those tutorials Mr. Stokes had mentioned.

I pretended to be scanning the book, but I couldn't help noticing Gabe, who was sitting across the aisle from me. Not that I was interested in meeting another boy just yet. But purely from a behavioral standpoint it was interesting to try to figure out what it was about him that made a tough cookie like Amelia melt all over. Bent down over his test paper, he looked like the standard issue boy to me. Maybe a little taller than usual and with dark eyebrows and sort of sun-bleached hair. I glanced around the room and realized that everybody looks pretty much alike when they're working on a test. They all hunch over mimeographed sheets, biting their lips with a glazed look in their eyes, and whatever makes them interesting is temporarily submerged beneath the boring part that works equations. I realized I was going to have to wait until Gabe looked up from the test if I wanted to find out what it was Amelia saw in him.

Most of the class took the whole period to finish the test, which I did not find encouraging. Then the bell rang, and people began flinging their papers on Mr. Stokes's desk and rushing out. Amelia showed up at my side with Christie, who was to take me to English class. I knew right away that I was going to like Christie better than Amelia, but then I'd met barracudas I liked better than Amelia. Christie was a short, plump girl who walked with a bounce. "I hope you're going to like the academy," she burbled as we left Chemistry class. "I just love it. Everybody's so nice. You've just got to come to the musicale Saturday night. I'm helping bake the cookies. Mr. Stokes is going to play the guitar."

"Mr. Stokes?" I said. "The Chemistry teacher?" I could imagine gypsies or aged hippies playing guitars, but not pale, stooped Mr. Stokes.

"Oh, yes," said Christie. "He plays super well. And he's just the nicest person. I just adore him. Have you had a chance to meet any kids yet?"

"Only Amelia," I said.

"Isn't she gorgeous? She should be a model! I wish I looked like that. She looks just positively terrific!"

"She didn't seem to be terrifically friendly," I said.

Christie suddenly dimpled. "Maybe she doesn't like competition," she said. "But really, Tish, you ought to come to the musicale. It's just a great place to meet people and it's going to be really nice."

"I just hope I can make it," I said. "It does sound really, really nice." Then I shook my head to clear it.

I never say things are "really nice." If I wasn't care-ful, I was going to end up talking just like Christie. I cleared my throat. "Uh, who teaches English?" I asked.

"Miss May," said Christie.

There was a silence, and it was then I felt the cold breath of doom at the back of my neck. In Miss May, evidently, Christie had finally found someone she didn't "just adore."

We walked together for a while without saying anything, then as we came up to Room 53, Christie said, "Well, here we are."

I wondered if I detected a note of queasiness in her voice. I found myself reluctant to step into the class-room and hesitated at the door. "Oh, I did meet one other person," I said to Christie. "I forgot to tell you, I met Bryan Something-or-other."

Christie lit up again. "Don't you just adore Bryan? He's so sweet. And did you meet his dog, Belle? She's amazing. So smart. Almost like a per-son. I just adore Labradors. They are the sweetest dogs."

I could see that Christie wasn't who you'd go to for incisive character analysis, but, on the other hand, it would be hard to find anybody more agree-able. It was comforting to know that she'd be going around tomorrow telling everybody that she just adored the new girl, Tish.

We went on into the classroom, and I saw that it was quite a small class. Only about ten kids. One of them was Gabe. I felt a momentary impulse to walk over to him and say, "This is a survey. Tell me why you are so fatally attractive to girls," but luckily I was able to control myself.

At first there was no sign of Miss May, but after I sat down, almost immediately she walked into the room. All chatter stopped, as when the shadow of a hawk falls on a twittering flock of sparrows.

She was an insignificant-looking little woman who had apparently tried to add to her height by heaping her colorless hair on top of her head. Several strands of it had come loose. In fact, her hair was done so ineptly she would have looked like a kid trying to dress like her older sister except that she was obviously no kid. She had a hooked nose and a totally negligible chin. The thing I noticed most, though, was that she was wearing open-toed shoes with a strap across the heels, and she couldn't seem to keep her heels in her shoe. They kept slipping and sliding off. Half the time her heels were dangling out of the shoe in thin air. I wondered why, if she had so much trouble managing strappy high heels, she didn't just wear flats. Maybe it was another way of trying to look taller or maybe she thought that kind of shoe was glamorous.

She looked at the class so sourly as she came in that I didn't have the courage to go up and introduce myself, but as it turned out, that wasn't necessary. As soon as the bell finished ringing, she spotted me. "Letitia Summerlin," she said, looking right at me. I began to feel hot. I had hoped to keep people from finding out my real name. I only use it on official things like my driver's license. "Mr. Morrison tells me you are exceptionally gifted in English," she said in the tones you would use to confront a check forger. "Humph," she added sourly, "we shall see."

My first impulse was to kill Daddy for feeding that "gifted" line to Mr. Morrison. My second impulse was to strangle Miss May. So what if I was good in English? There was nothing wrong with that. I had been at the academy all morning, and I had just about had enough of being humble. First Amelia had frozen me with her cold smile, then I had been mesmerized by the sight of a herd of blazers the combined worth of which probably equalled the gross national product of many an African country. Now Miss May was giving me a look that would have curdled milk just because I was good in English. Well, I'm not going to quiver at her glance, I thought. I sat up straighter and looked her right in the eye. At last, I had the pleasure of seeing her look away to shuffle the papers on her desk. No doubt she had a guilty conscience.

I didn't say anything during the class because it was all a lecture by Miss May. I had to admit that she certainly knew a lot about the Romantic poets, but she was one of those people who didn't believe in class discussion, and when she left off talking about the poets' scandalous personal lives and started reading "Ode to Melancholy" aloud I had to fight a desire to doze off.

Once class was over, everybody scooted out of the room very quickly. I guessed they were eager to get out of Miss May's reach. I was as fast on my feet as the rest of them. but the whole class had elbowed past Christie, so I had to wait for her. As Gabe passed me he grinned and called to me, "Hey, it's nothing personal. She hates us all."

Suddenly, I thought I saw what it was about Gabe that made Amelia melt. He had a very assured, almost arrogant way about him, yet he smiled at you as if he had decided he liked you most especially. I could see how that smile would take him far, even with a girl like Amelia.

Christie finally got out of the classroom, and then I had to hurry to keep up with her.

"Whew," I said. "Is Miss May always like that?"

She struggled for a minute between wanting to assure me that Miss May was perfectly adorable and knowing I could see for myself that she wasn't. "She's strict," she hedged.

"She's awful," I said. "That's what."

But as we got farther away from the classroom the bounce came back into Christie's step. "The rest of the teachers aren't a bit like her," she assured me. "You're just going to love them."

By the end of the school day, I was exhausted from trying to match new faces with new names and trying to figure out where I was going to fit into it all. But I had decided that Christie was right. The rest of the teachers did seem nice. Miss May was just one of those miscellaneous unpleasant things you had to put up with, like cold feet or mosquitoes. She was bad, but the rest of the school seemed pretty much okay, so I figured I'd survive.

After school, Blake picked me up in front of the school as we had arranged. At that point, I was glad to see a familiar face. Only later did it occur to me that he had arranged to pick me up in front of the school in hopes of keeping the kids at the parking lot from figuring out we were related.

After we had been driving a couple of minutes in silence, I finally said, "Well, aren't you going to ask me how my day went?"

He looked at me in astonishment. "Tish, you know I don't care how your day went. I just want you to stay out of my hair."

Nobody could say Blake wasn't honest. "It went fine," I said. "I think I'm going to like the academy."

"Sorry to hear that," he said.

"Why do you have to be so mean?" I said. "Do you think you're the only person in the world? Other people have feelings."

"Why do you have to follow me around?" he said. "What was wrong with Senior High? You were doing fine there, but no, you had to follow me around."

"I like that!" I said. "I have just as much right to be at the academy as you do."

We were still fighting when we got home and walked into the house.

"Just live your own life," Blake was shouting as we came into the kitchen, "and leave me out of it."

"Don't worry," I said bitterly. "I don't want anybody to know I'm related to you either."

"Stop it, both of you," Mom said. "How was your day, Tish?"

"Great," I said. "It was terrific. I'm going to love the academy. And I'm going to stay there whether Blake likes it or not."

"That's nice, dear," said Mom. "Want a cookie?"

Blake went into his room and slammed the door, but I sat down at the table and tried to act civilized. That, of course, was because I was a nice person and Blake was not. "Sure," I said.

I suddenly had a pleasant thought. I had gone through an entire day and had scarcely thought about Mike and Mimsy at all. This showed that I had done the right thing to transfer to the academy. Even if I did have to ride over there in the same car as Blake and put up with Miss May besides. Naturally, there would be a few bumps and jolts as I was getting used to the new school, but probably it would work out fine in the end. Who knows? I thought as I bit into the cookie. Maybe Miss May won't be so bad once I get to know her.

Chapter Three

My hopes that Miss May wouldn't turn out to be so bad were soon dashed. It took no time at all for the two of us to move to open warfare. One day I was an average, happy-go-lucky high school student, trying to catch up in Chemistry and working on an English theme for Thursday, and the next day I was wondering how much time I'd spend in jail for firebombing Miss May's apartment.

I have always been good at writing themes. One of the reasons for that is that I slave over them for hours. I worked extra hard on this one because I had the feeling that if anything was wrong with it, Miss May would hold it up in class for people to laugh at and would make sarcastic comments about my being "gifted" in English. I didn't want to give her the pleasure.

I handed it in on Thursday, and Friday morning, when we filed into class, Miss May handed it back. It had a zero on it. Not a C- or a D or an F, but a plain, flat zero. When my vision cleared, I saw that at the top of the paper was written in red the simple comment "No name." I flipped through the paper and saw that there wasn't a single other red mark. Miss May had given me a zero because I forgot to put my name on the paper! It was so unfair it took my breath away. It wasn't as if she didn't know who the paper belonged to. Our class was small and she had handed it right to me.

When I thought about what a zero would do to my grade average, my fingers felt cold. I expect the shock had done something awful to my circulatory system. I had never gotten a zero in my whole life. I had never even known anyone who got a zero. Once I knew somebody who got a ten on a pop quiz on the rivers of North Carolina, but not even the dumbest people I knew got zeros. Zeros were what people got for major crimes like plagiarizing. I darted a glance up front at Miss May and caught her looking at me, a faint smile on her lips. She was really an awful woman.

I didn't want to let her know how upset I was, but angry tears stung my eyes and I could almost feel my nose going red and shiny. I did hear her say, "Today, class, we will be taking a brief look at the development of the novel," but after that the class was sort of a blur. My mind was too full of that zero for me to make sense out of anything else.

As soon as class was over, I got out of there fast. I was afraid if I got too close to Miss May, I might strangle her, and I knew that wouldn't look very good on my permanent record.

The rest of the day I had a terrible time concentrating. In American History I heard Mrs. Lewis say, "Tish?" and I came to with a start. "I've called your name three times!" she said. "Are you asleep?"

"I'm sorry," I said, blushing. "I didn't hear you."

The more I brooded about that zero, the more I became convinced that Miss May was out for my blood. I didn't for a minute believe that she gave zeros to all the kids who ever forgot to put their names on their papers. She was out to get me. But what could I do about it? Nothing, unfortunately. My position was very sticky.

I couldn't very well transfer back to Senior High to escape her clutches. Transferring twice in one week would make me look like a complete and utter fruitcake. Besides, I knew that Mom and Dad had to pay my tuition for the semester in advance, and it wasn't very likely they would be sympathetic with my not sticking around to make use of an education they had already paid for. I only had to think about how weird they were about using up leftover broccoli to see which way that argument would go. There was no way out.

In some families all I'd have to do would be to bring that zero home, and the parents would be laying siege to the administration building and demanding Miss May's head on a plate. But, unfortunately, my family wasn't like that. They were the types who were always saying things like "Look at it from their side" and "You'll just have to get used to their little prejudices, dear." I had heard those lines a thousand times. And I could still remember the time Blake's fifth grade teacher had hauled off and socked him in the jaw. Admittedly, in Blake's case you could see that the teacher probably had provocation. But while the other parents had been gathering names on a petition, and while the Committee Against Violence in Our Schools had been laying the groundwork for a suit, my parents were still saying, "Let's give the man another chance." I knew I wasn't going to get any help from them.

All day I was in a daze. When school was over, I didn't dash out front as usual to catch my ride home with Blake. I had decided to wait until he had gone and then to walk home. I remembered reading somewhere that walking pumped extra oxygen to the brain and helped promote good ideas. I figured I could use a good idea.

While the other kids streamed from the classroom buildings to the parking lot where their late model cars awaited them, I made my way to a little garden next to the east classroom wing. The school catalog called it "a garden for quiet meditation" and actually showed some kids meditating in it, something I hadn't seen yet. I supposed November wasn't the high season for outdoor meditation.

It was not exactly a beautiful garden. A low brick wall, some bushes, and a willow tree enclosed the place, and in one corner someone had left a garbage can overflowing with old leaves and branches. Along the wall there were some scraggly chrysanthemums turning brown, and in the middle, a fountain gurgled over a sodden gum wrapper. It was a very depressing place. The one thing that could be said for it was that it suited my mood perfectly. I sat down on a cold bench to wait until Blake drove off. Knowing him the way I did, I knew it wouldn't be a long wait. The minute he saw I wasn't at our meeting place, I was sure he would take off.

I sat there listening to the gurgling fountain and wishing I lived in a better world, a world where I didn't have to watch Mike nuzzling Mimsy and where I didn't have to put up with that troll, Miss May. I had read somewhere that the famous writer William Faulkner once drew a map of the imaginary place where his stories took place, Yoknapatawpha County, and in the corner of the map he had written "Yoknapatawpha County: William Faulkner, proprietor." That was the kind of world I needed, I thought, the kind I owned and ran myself. Wouldn't it be lovely to be in a place where I was in charge and Miss May counted for zilch? The trouble was in the real world, Miss May was in charge, and I was the one who counted for zilch. It was only in song and story that the good guy won all the battles.

I wondered if I could make up a jingle in which Miss May got her just deserts. It wouldn't be as good as being proprietor of the real world, but it might make me feel a little better.

"My dear Miss May, come in, my sweet," I muttered to myself, trying out a sample line. "Miss May" was an easy name to work with, much easier than "Mrs. Cladiddlehopper," for example. While I stared at the dripping fountain, lines seemed to file obligingly into my mind. A little rearranging and re-shuffling was all they needed. I had been rubbing my hands together to keep them warm, but in a minute or two I had quit being conscious of my cold hands, and I thought I had the jingle. I decided to test it out loud and see how it sounded. In fact, for a second there I was so pleased with it, I felt like dancing to it. I purred venomously:

> My dear Miss May, come in, my sweet,
>   A fine revenge awaits you.
>   Come listen to the heartfelt wish
>   Of someone here who hates you.
>   Please step into this garbage can,
>   I'll fill you full of arrows,
>   I'll trim your nose and plump your chin
>   And stick some extra arrows in
>   And bang your head once and again
>   Until it shrinks and narrows.

Heh, heh, I thought. That last line was a little forced, but on the whole not bad. It had a nice snarly sound that I liked. I went on more quickly.

I'll hang you from your silly heels.
And now listen to *me* crow.
It's time for you to get your grade.
Miss May, you get a *zero!*

I folded my arms in satisfaction. Not bad, I thought. Not bad at all. Feeling sort of nice and warm with hate, I reached to gather up my books from the bench beside me, then suddenly I jumped. Someone behind me was clapping!

I wheeled around. It was Gabe! I was relieved to see that it wasn't Miss May, but I could still feel myself blushing. I have always had a real problem with blushing.

"I thought maybe you were going to string her up the tree," he said.

"I did," I said. "By her heels. I don't want her dead. I just want to see her suffer." I picked up my books and stood up. It was embarrassing to be caught reciting rhymes out loud. Even more important, I didn't like for a perfect stranger to find out how much Miss May got to me.

Without another word I hurried out of the garden, the pebbles of the path crunching under my feet. As I came out of the garden I saw Blake in Mom's car speeding away down the street in front.

"Looks like you missed your ride," said Gabe, coming up beside me.

"I wanted to walk anyway," I said.

He raised an eyebrow at me. I supposed walking was considered weird in the Porsche and Cadillac world of the academy.

"It's not all that far," I said. Then I realized that if he knew Blake, he might know where we lived and would see that, by the standards of anybody except a world-class hiker, it was a fair distance.

"I'll keep you company," he said. "I live in that direction, too."

I couldn't very well tell him to go away and leave me alone, so I just started walking. Perhaps, I thought, I will say something frivolous just to show how basically easygoing I am. The only problem was that I was still so mad at Miss May, I was afraid if I said something frivolous I would choke on it.

"What did Miss May do to you?" he asked, shortening his stride to stay in step with me.

"She gave me a zero on my theme because I forgot to put my name on it," I said. I realized that my speaking through clenched teeth must be somewhat undercutting my efforts to appear easygoing.

There was a moment's silence while I ground my teeth.

"I don't guess she mentioned that you get to drop your lowest grade," he said.

I looked at him in astonishment. "No!" I said. "No, she didn't."

"It's come in handy for me already," he said. "Last six weeks she gave me an F on my class participation."

"She did? An F!" I gasped. "How could she do that?" I was appalled. Here was another danger to be sidestepped.

"She said I had a rotten attitude."

"I think it's great you take it so well."

"Heck, I don't take it well," he said. "If I could pull out her silly little toenails one by one, it'd be a pleasure. She knows I need a nice fat scholarship for college. I can't let my grades slip. It's no secret I'm at the academy on scholarship."

I was pretty wrapped up in my own troubles, but the tinge of bitterness in Gabe's voice was strong enough for even me to notice. I began to feel a little less embarrassed about his having caught me reciting my nasty little poem. It didn't look as if he were exactly easygoing himself.

"Whatever can be the matter with her!" I said. "Why does she have to act like this?"

"I have a theory," he said. "I figure it's actually a compliment for her to be after your skin. The more you seem to be on top of things, the more she wants to slit your throat."

"That's a fine attitude," I said hotly. "I thought teachers were supposed to want for you to do well."

"Not Miss May," he said. "To get through her class it helps to be a little dumb and to grovel a lot."

There was a long silence after that. I was thinking I wouldn't be very good at groveling. On top of having trouble being easygoing, I had a slight problem with pride. Maybe I could trade in my whole personality and get a new one. I was not making out too well with this one.

"She likes to help people," Gabe said.

I looked at him with astonishment. "She likes to *help* people?"

"Yeah, She likes for you to have something really wrong with you so she can help you." He went on with relish. "You see, my theory is that she likes people best if they're ugly or crippled or wasting away with some terrible disease or something. Then she can help them."

"That is so sick," I said, appalled.

"Take Bryan," Gabe went on cheerfully. "She's nuts about Bryan. It's disgusting. It even turns him off. Bring me the lame, the halt, the blind—that's her. She's crazy about people with some big problem so she can feel superior. What she can't stand is for you to feel too good or look too sure of yourself."

For a mad moment I wondered if I could borrow Dad's wheelchair. If Gabe was right about Miss May, I had been doomed for the start. First, I had come into class labeled "gifted" and then right off I had stared her down. I could imagine how she'd made a little black mark next to my name with the notation "marked for destruction."

"I wish this kind of thing didn't get to me," I moaned. "I wish I could just laugh it off."

"Miss May is a hard one to laugh off," he said. He stopped walking. "This is my house," he said. "So long." He smiled, then turned down the driveway to his house. I watched as he walked away, radiating self-confidence, just asking Miss May to slap him down.

Gabe's house was one of the modest little frame structures left over from the days before the developers named the neighborhood Ravenwood and started trying to fill it with broad lawns and high-income types. The house was a poky, beat-up-looking place with slightly mildewed asbestos shingles and green shutters. A small garage at the end of the muddy driveway had a sign on it saying FIX-IT SHOP and the mailbox carried a neat little placard saying AGNES FARRAR, SEAMSTRESS. ALTERATIONS, MONOGRAMS. It looked as if Gabe's whole family was working at odd jobs.

It must seem funny, I thought, to be working hard to make ends meet at home and at the same time to be going to the academy with all those rich kids. I knew how being surrounded by those expensive blazers had gotten to me, and Gabe's family was obviously more strapped for funds than we were. But however Gabe might feel about the academy and Miss May, it obviously hadn't done anything to squelch him. Even the way he walked, with that careless, long stride, looked somehow triumphant. If Miss May didn't like self-confidence, Gabe must positively drive her nuts.

I walked on in the direction of my own house feeling a bit better. The news that I'd be able to drop my lowest grade had done a lot for my mood. My situation was still sticky. Miss May could easily give me an F on attitude the way she had Gabe, for instance. But at least there was hope. Maybe I would somehow manage to avoid falling into her clutches again. Maybe I could spend ten minutes a night in front of my mirror practicing groveling. At the very least, I could certainly be careful to put my name on my papers.

It cheered me up a bit, too, to see that I wasn't the only kid she'd gotten her teeth into. She was after

Gabe, too, and he was just as mad at her as I was. I figured that if I should ever take to the hills to begin guerrilla action against Miss May I could count on him joining my band. I wondered when I'd get the chance to talk to him again.

Chapter Four

The next evening was the musicale at school and I borrowed Mom's car for it. When Blake found out that the keys were missing from the key rack and that I had them, he howled like a banshee. "Tish has the car?" he bellowed indignantly. "What am I supposed to do? I was going to meet Jason at the pizza place."

Mom said, "Tish asked for the car days ago. You're going to have to learn to arrange these things with me ahead of time."

Blake shot a speculative look at Dad. "Don't look at me," Dad said. "I'm using my car. I've got a Human Relations Committee meeting at eight."

"Why don't you see if Jason can pick you up," Mom suggested. "Now that Tish has her license, you two are going to have to learn to share the car. And don't forget that I might like to use it myself now and then."

This time we both looked at her with panic. Things were really going to be tight with the car if Mom started using it herself.

"It's not fair," Blake protested automatically, but his mind was already churning and plotting his next move. Suddenly he said, "I want to put in a standing order for the car every Saturday night."

"Hey, wait a minute!" I said.

"Girls aren't supposed to need cars on Saturday night," he said quickly. "They're supposed to be sharp enough to get guys to take them places."

"You are a joke, Blake," I said hotly. "You really are."

"I hope," Dad said, "we are not going to have to take away everybody's car privileges in order to keep peace in this family."

That shut us both up and we had to content ourselves with nasty looks. Then suddenly I caught a glimpse of the clock and grabbed at the keys. "Oh, my gosh," I said. "I'm going to be late."

I rushed out, leaving Blake behind me, keening for the lost car. I was excited about going to the musicale. I was really hoping I might see Gabe there. Even if he weren't there, I hoped *somebody* I recognized would be, maybe Christie.

When I got to the school, I could tell I was late because the circular driveway in front was lined with cars. I found the common room, a kind of lounge near the office, pushed open the door, and went in.

The room was dimly lit, and at first I couldn't make out the faces of the kids who were sitting around on the furniture and all over the floor. The only light in the room was shining on Mr. Stokes, who was sitting on a tall stool in the center of the room, playing the guitar very fast in a Spanish-sounding way. I found a patch of floor near the couch and sat down. I strained my eyes looking around the room, but saw no sign of Gabe. Suddenly, I got quite a start when a furry face turned toward me in the gloom. The person sitting next to me turned out to be no person at all but Belle, the Labrador retriever. She had a habit of turning up in the most unexpected places. I found it unnerving to be going along peacefully under the vague impression that everybody in the crowd was a fellow human being and to suddenly meet with a black snout and a cold, wet nose. I could see that Bryan was next to her, on a footstool.

In a few minutes Mr. Stokes finished playing the Spanish music and began talking about the work pioneering musicologists had done collecting folk music. I supposed this was the cultural enrichment my father had been talking about. I found it somewhat less exciting than a football game.

After he had filled us in on musicologists, Mr. Stokes began singing about dark nights, unquiet graves, black-hearted lovers, and unrequited love. He peered nearsightedly into the dim room, the light reflecting off his rimless glasses and giving him a blank look like Little Orphan Annie. It was hard to connect him with unrequited love. He looked like a person more suited to filling out income tax returns, somehow, than falling in love. But then I supposed I looked ordinary enough, too, and look what unrequited love had driven me to. True, I didn't go around drawing daggers and singing "Thou shalt ne'er another love," in a minor key the way those people in songs did, but I had transferred to a different school, and that was a pretty drastic step. At least I thought so.

After Mr. Stokes had sufficiently gorged himself on gloom, and when the body count of the songs had become alarming, he put down his guitar to take a break. Kids began getting up and drifting over to the table where cookies and punch were being dispensed. I reached over and touched Bryan's hand. "Want some cookies, Bryan?" I said. "I could bring some back for you, if you want." He looked right at me. I sensed he didn't like it that he couldn't place my voice, but didn't like to say so. He had a slight crease between his eyebrows, but he smiled. "Thanks. I like anything with chocolate in it."

Belle gave me a hostile look as I got up and made my way over to the cookies. She was a big dog, and I decided I'd better bring her a couple of cookies, too, to be sure of getting on her right side. I came back to my place, balancing the plates of cookies on top of the cups of cocoa.

I put my own stuff down, very gingerly, and handed Bryan his. "Okay," I said, "here they are. Chocolate only." I sat down again and put the plate of cookies on my knees. "I'm Tish," I told him. "We met in home room on Monday. This is my first week at the academy."

"Hi, Tish," he said. I noticed he had a low, kind of grainy voice with a lot of warmth in it. Belle gave me a nasty look, and I quickly fed her my two choicest cookies.

"I don't think Belle likes me," I said nervously.

Bryan laughed. "She thinks she has to protect me," he said. "Do you have any more of the ones with the chocolate sprinkles on them? I'd trade you for one of mine."

"Sure," I said. I gave him a chocolate-sprinkled one. He took my hand and somehow it ended up staying in his while we talked. If anyone else had parlayed a cookie into a hand-holding session in the first conversation, I would have figured he was a fast worker, but with Bryan it seemed more like his way of keeping in touch, the way another person might look at your face while you talked. I noticed he had thick, blunt-looking hands and wore a heavy signet ring that glinted in the dim light.

"So what do you think of the academy so far?" he asked.

"I haven't really learned my way around yet," I said.

"It takes a while," he said.

Just then Belle pushed her head up between us, and Bryan had to let go of my hand to tousle her head.

"Nice doggie," I said uneasily.

"She's a great girl," said Bryan. "I got her the summer before last. We went to school together to learn to work with each other."

Belle smiled at me and I noticed what strong, white, sharp teeth she had, reminding one of some of the more sinister scenes in *Little Red Riding Hood*. I got the distinct impression that she didn't like me being too friendly with Bryan. I supposed she was jealous. Of course, I had heard of romantic triangles, but boy-girl-dog?

"I think Belle doesn't like me," I said to Bryan.

"Belle?" He smiled. "Nah. Why, where she was trained, they said she had the best temperament of any of the dogs in her class! She's a sweetie."

I wondered what else was in her class. Doberman pinscher attack dogs, probably.

"Why don't you give me your phone number, Tish," said Bryan.

To my surprise, he pulled a little black address book out of one pocket.

"Okay," I said. I turned to the S's and wrote in my name, address and phone number. The name at the top of the page was Dr. Simmons, dentist, and curiously I saw that his name was dotted with tiny holes, as if someone had gone after the address book with an ice pick. It hit me then that the addresses in the book must have been translated into braille by somebody. I would have loved to get a closer look at it, but suddenly Mr. Stokes appeared again and took up his guitar. I hastily finished scrawling my address and handed it back to Bryan.

"And now for some pieces in the classical tradition," said Mr. Stokes.

I was glad I had gotten plenty of sleep the night before, because I had the suspicion that staying awake during this bunch of pieces was going to be tough. Luckily, I did have some other things to occupy my mind, like wondering what sort of person Bryan was. I had noticed something interesting about him while we had been holding hands. His arms were unusually muscular and you could see the veins in them. I decided he must lift weights. Most blind kids probably found enough challenge in just getting across streets without getting hit by a car, but evidently that wasn't enough for Bryan. He must go out in the garage and pump iron on top of it all. Underneath those smiles, he had to be a pretty driven kind of person.

I decided he must like me, or else why would he have gotten my phone number? I was glad he seemed to take to me, because after the battering my ego had taken when Mike dumped me, I needed all the approval I could get. But the person I really wanted to see was Gabe. Where was he? There was no sign of him and I found myself being ridiculously disappointed.

After the musicale, as all the kids were streaming out of the common room, Christie appeared out of the crowd, waved at me enthusiastically, and bounced over to me. I was glad to see her. After an uncomfortable hour spent looking at Belle's sharp teeth I was in the mood for sweetness.

"Tish," she squealed. "I'm so glad you made it. Didn't you think it was just super? I didn't see you in there. Did you get to meet any people?"

"Uh, sure," I said. After all, I thought, I had talked to Bryan. It was a start.

"Oh, terrific!" said Christie. "Didn't I tell you this was a super place to meet people?"

I might not have been meeting as many people as Christie, in her boundless optimism, thought, but as it turned out, Bryan lost no time making use of my phone number. The very next night he called me up and asked me to go to the movies. I would have loved to know if his dog, Belle, was coming along, but I didn't like to ask.

I gave Stephanie a full report on my progress at the academy when she called, later the same night.

"How's life among the rich?" she asked breathlessly. "Have you met any kids yet? What are they like?"

"It seems okay, so far," I said. "At first all the kids looked alike to me because most of them wear those matching navy-blue blazers, but I've started being able to tell them apart. So far most people seem pretty friendly. I've even got a date for Friday night already."

"No kidding!"

"With Bryan Guthrie. Do you know him?"

"I don't think so. What's he like?"

"I haven't got to know him very well yet. All I know is that he's blind, he has a Seeing Eye dog named Belle, he drives a Lincoln Continental, and we're going to the movie together Friday night."

There was a moment of silence. "Wait a minute," said Stephanie. "Did you say he was blind?"

"That's right."

"Well, then how can he drive a Lincoln Continental, and why are you two going to the movies?"

"I don't know, Steph. Those questions don't even occur to me when I'm talking to him. He just acts as if he's got everything under control." I paused. "There is one thing worrying me, though. That dog. His Seeing Eye dog. I don't think she likes me. I think she wants him all to herself."

"It's probably your imagination," said Stephanie.

I shivered. "You should see the looks she gives me."

Stephanie giggled. "Well, if you can't compete with a dog, you're in bad shape."

"Very funny. I bet you wouldn't like to have a chaperon with two-inch teeth."

"Be firm. Show her who's boss."

I maintained a dubious silence.

"Well," she said, "do you want to hear any news from your old school?"

"I'm not sure," I said cautiously. "What kind of news?"

"Well, the band's been invited to Washington to play in the Festival of States parade."

"That's nice," I said. I couldn't believe she had called me up just to warn me that the band was going to be engaging in a frenzy of candy-selling to pay for a trip to Washington. "Anything else?" I said.

"Well..." she said, pausing dramatically, "Mike and Mimsy got called into the principal's office and warned against public displays of affection."

"I got out of there just in time, Steph," I said fervently. "Honestly."

"You don't see the funny side of it?"

"No," I said, "I do not."

"I wish you didn't have to take things so hard," she said. "Everybody else thought it was hilarious."

I groaned.

"So you're really glad you transferred, huh?"

"Yup."

"And you're still really upset about Mike dumping you, huh?'

I supposed it would have been more romantic to say that I would bear the scars of my broken romance forever, but I realized it wouldn't be true. Now that I didn't have to see Mike and Mimsy mooning over each other, I was feeling a hundred percent better. In fact, I was spending a lot of time daydreaming about Gabe. It certainly showed that one of the things that had gotten me down about Mike throwing me over was the humiliation of it. To realize that he didn't even care enough about my feelings to save his and Mimsy's demonstrations of affection for private had been the crowning blow to my pride.

"If I just don't have to see them together, I get along okay," I said.

"That's good," said Stephanie. "But moving to another school seems like kind of an extreme way of coping to me."

Thinking of the troubles I had run into at the academy, like Miss May's zero and Belle's long teeth, I had to agree.

My second week at the academy whizzed by. I wasn't going to be able to join in the chamber music ensemble because the Chemistry tutorial was at the same time. On the other hand, I did have some hope of catching up with Chemistry before Christmas, so maybe I could join the group later.

Miss May droned her way through the early English novelists with so little enthusiasm in her voice, she sounded like the steady hum of an air conditioner. I took notes like mad so I wouldn't have to look her in the eye. In my margins I doodled sketches of knives, nooses, submachine guns, and hand grenades. Sometimes I doodled sketches of Miss May with an arrow through her head. I certainly was glad the school psychologist couldn't see those margins, but doing them made me feel a lot better.

Friday night, I did my best to put my problems with Miss May out of my mind, and I got all dressed up for my date with Bryan. Remembering that he couldn't see my dress, I squirted on lots of Mom's best perfume, too.

Mom was at a meeting for the American Association of University Women, and Dad was at the board meeting for Friends of the Library, so to my relief neither of them were around to check out Bryan when he arrived. My parents were famous for giving my dates the third degree. They would be back by the time we came in, and I knew they'd give him the third degree then, but I could worry about that later. Meanwhile, when the doorbell rang I was able to go to the door with a light heart, for a change.

I opened the door and was staggered to find Gabe standing on the doorstep instead of Bryan. The light at the front door cast his eyes in shadow and glimmered on his hair, which looked as if it had been combed damp. For a second it was like a dream. I had been wishing it was Gabe coming for me instead of Bryan, then suddenly there he was!

"Bryan's in the car," he said. "I came up to get you."

My heart did a little plop of disappointment. Of course, I had known there must be a simple explanation for Gabe's being there, but I suppose some little part of me must have still believed in magic, or I wouldn't have felt so downhearted at his announcement that Bryan was waiting.

"I work as Bryan's reader," he said as we walked out to the car. "That means I read his school assignments to him. And it works out that lots of times we double."

So Gabe was Bryan's reader. I hadn't thought about it before, but of course he would need one unless his parents had the time to read aloud for him. Obviously, not all textbooks came in braille or on cassettes.

Gabe stepped right over the azalea bushes and got in the driver's seat, but I walked around them in order to preserve my stockings. When I opened the car door the inside car light switched on, and I could see Bryan in the back seat. There was no sign of Belle, and I cheered up a little as I realized he hadn't brought her with him. I slid in next to him and touched his hand in greeting. "Hi," I said.

"Hi, there," he smiled, squeezing my hand.

Then the girl sitting next to Gabe in the front seat turned around, and I saw to my dismay that it was Amelia. "Hi, Tish," she said cosily.

I gasped. As far as I was concerned, having Amelia around was just about as bad as having Bryan's dog around. In fact, Amelia reminded me a lot of Belle. They both had those glittering teeth and that menacing smile.

I choked out some greeting, then Gabe started the big car and it began to move, smoothly and silently like a ship. I expected this was what it was like to ride in the President's limousine. Utter luxury and comfort. All we needed was the Secret Service men and the bulletproof glass to complete the effect. I decided Bryan must be one of the rich kids I had thought the academy would be full of.

"Cold night," said Bryan, squeezing my hand.

"They say they're going to get snow in the mountains," said Amelia.

Our part of North Carolina hardly ever gets any snow but that doesn't stop people from talking about the possibility in boring detail all the way from November to April.

"Probably we'll just get rain here," said Bryan, "unless we get a few flurries in the morning."

I was morbidly conscious that Amelia was sitting next to Gabe in the front seat. In fact, she was so close to him I didn't see how she could possibly be wearing a seat belt.

"I hear this is supposed to be a bad winter," I gulped. It had been a while since I had been on a first date, and I was a little afraid I had lost the knack of talking about the weather, but I was willing to give it a try.

"Yeah," said Gabe, "I heard that. The woolly worms are digging themselves in deep, they say, and the squirrels are putting away twenty-five percent more nuts than last year. Of course, the really important thing is the groundhogs, and I don't think the reports are in on them yet."

Amelia looked at Gabe in bewilderment. "But how do they know where to look for the nuts the squirrels hide?"

"ESP," said Gabe. "That's extra squirrelly perception." But then he glanced at her and saw she wasn't smiling. "They don't really," he said gently. "I was just kidding."

"Oh," she said, the corners of her mouth settling into a discontented line.

When we got to the movie theater and Amelia got out of the car, I could see she was wearing tight black silk pants with zippers all over the place and a matching Windbreaker. A rush of winter wind blew her shiny hair across her face and she smiled broadly, flashing white teeth. She looked exactly the way a Doberman pinscher would look if it had been reincarnated as a girl. I, personally, did not see the attraction, but then, I thought, there's no accounting for the tastes of boys, as I should have known by now. I took Bryan's hand and we got out, too, following Gabe and Amelia disguised as a paratrooper.

I have always hated being conspicuous. The big ambition of my life has been to blend into the crowd.

So what was I doing going to the movie in the company of a blind person and a beautiful paratrooper? We naturally drew all eyes to us. When we got up to the ticket booth, the woman behind the counter couldn't take her eyes off Bryan in his distinctive wraparound dark glasses. I could see that being conspicuous didn't bother Amelia. In the light that fanned out from the ticket booth, she clung to Gabe's arm, tossing her hair and flashing her white teeth as if she expected a talent scout to step forward and claim her for stardom.

Oh, well, I thought stoically. This is the sort of evening that builds a person's character. Think of pioneers crossing the frozen prairie, of mountain climbers following their Sherpa guides through blinding blizzards. If they could keep going, Tish old girl, so can you.

I was glad, though, when we stepped into the lobby. We didn't seem so noticeable in the milling crowd in front of the popcorn machine. Bryan pulled out a bill to pay for the popcorn and I saw that it was a five, folded triangularly. Each denomination of bill must be folded in a different way so he could tell them apart. Amelia held out her hand to check the condition of the nail polish on her talons, then flashed a smile at Gabe as he handed her a box of popcorn. I felt slightly sick and took another moment to wonder what Gabe could see in Amelia. Outside, that is, of her being beautiful and obviously crazy about him.

Bryan handed me my popcorn and put his arm around my waist. "You're awfully quiet," he murmured in my ear. "A penny for your thoughts."

I couldn't very well tell him I was thinking about Gabe and Amelia. "Miss May," I said desperately. In one way that was true. I was always thinking about Miss May—how to get back at her, how to escape her, how to stop thinking about her.

"Let's don't think about Miss May tonight," he murmured.

"You don't like her either?" I said.

"Nobody likes her," he said. "Hey, Gabe, have you ever heard of anybody liking Miss May?"

"Well, there was that concentration camp guard back in '43," said Gabe. "The two of them had a lot in common."

Amelia wrinkled her pretty brow. "But that was over forty years ago. She can't be that old. Are you sure you got the date right?"

"Just a little joke," explained Gabe. "Not a very good one."

"Oh," said Amelia.

I was beginning to conclude that light banter was not Amelia's strength. Not that I was coming across as wit of the year either. I was a little preoccupied with thinking about Gabe and how I wished he would fall desperately, madly, hopelessly in love with me or at least ask me out for a sandwich or something. In spite of these crazy thoughts I managed somehow to go on eating popcorn.

We filed into the darkened movie theater. The movie turned out to be about a big jewel heist. You almost couldn't have picked a worse movie for Bryan. It was full of scenes which consisted of nothing but gloved fingers moving on combination locks, people creeping soundlessly through dark rooms, heavy breathing, and things like that. I had to lean close to Bryan and keep up a running commentary in his ear so he could follow what was going on. "They're past the watchdogs now," I said. "Now they're crossing the courtyard. Oh, wait a minute, here comes a searchlight. But it's okay. They've scooted out of its reach."

"You're good at this," Bryan said. "You could write screenplays."

I smiled, then remembered to translate the smile into a squeeze. Bryan was a nice guy. It was too bad I kept hearing little giggles from Amelia and wondering what Gabe and Amelia were up to. It sort of interfered with my concentration.

After the movie, we all piled again into Bryan's car. I burrowed back into the deep plush of the back seat and brooded. I was not very happy. I would have preferred to be in the front seat with Gabe. You are a perverse personality, I lectured myself firmly. Whatever you have, you want something else. You will never be happy if you keep this up.

"First stop is Amelia's house," said Gabe, turning on the ignition. In the dim light cast by the instrument panel I could make out that Amelia's mouth had once more settled into a discontented line. Since the car belonged to Bryan and Gabe was only Bryan's chauffeur, there was obviously no way in the world that Amelia was ever going to get to be

alone with Gabe in it, but I could tell she hadn't resigned herself to that. She cast a nasty glance back at
Bryan and me. Bryan couldn't see it, of course, but
I could, and I knew that if Amelia had had the pow-
ers of a witch, Bryan and I would have been turned
into frogs that minute. As soon as I realized that, I
felt more cheerful. It may not be very nice to be
cheerful about the bad luck of your enemies, but it
beats not being cheerful at all.

Amelia's house turned out to be like a mansion,
only larger. Gabe walked her up to the front door. I
didn't see whether he kissed her good night or not. I
didn't want to see. I turned to Bryan with sudden
animation. "Did you notice," I said, "that they
never did explain in that movie how the gypsy's
dancing bear happened to get loose?"

"I guess there were some loose ends," Bryan admitted.

"And another thing," I said quickly, "nobody
ever explained why the lighthouse-keeper's daughter squealed on them."

Gabe was getting back in the car. At least his farewell to Amelia had been short. "No loyalty," he put
in. "She was just a sneaking, sniveling bit of skirt
with no loyalty."

Suddenly I felt transfixed with guilt. Here I was,
full of popcorn bought with Bryan's money, sitting
in Bryan's car, and wishing I were up front with
Gabe. That was not only disloyal, it wasn't even
plain, ordinary, everyday, basic nice. I felt awful.

When we got to my house, all three of us had to
walk up to the front door together. Gabe naturally

had to go with Bryan and me because since Bryan didn't have his dog with him, somebody had to walk with him back to the car and keep him from tripping over the azaleas.

Mom and Dad both came to the door to meet us. They looked a little surprised to see Gabe standing there. Of course, I had told them that Bryan was blind, but they hadn't totaled up all the inconveniences this meant.

"Come in, boys," Dad said. "Tish's mom has made some cocoa."

Bryan looked down at where Dad's voice was coming from, as was his habit, and puzzled furrows formed between his brows.

"My dad is not a midget, Bryan," I explained. "He uses a wheelchair."

"How was the movie?" said Dad, as he wheeled into the living room.

I was sure that the last thing Bryan and Gabe wanted to do was to sit on the couch and drink cocoa while my parents cross-examined Bryan and rated his ambition and the soundness of his values, but they seemed to sense there was no way out of it and filed meekly in to sit down on the couch.

"Thanks to Tish's excellent commentary, the movie was fine, sir," said Bryan.

"Tish has a way with words," Dad began, but I gave him a stern look and willed him not to brag about my SAT scores and after a glance at me he quickly veered to another subject. "Do you think we're going to get any snow tonight?" he said.

"Twenty percent chance, I believe the forecasters are saying, sir," said Bryan.

Mom came in with a tray of cocoa. If she started talking about snow, I felt I just might scream. As far as I was concerned, the conversational possibilities of snow had been fully and completely explored.

"How do you boys like the academy?" she said, putting the cocoa on the coffee table. "Do you think it's giving you good preparation for college?"

Bryan said, "I think so, Mrs. Summerlin. It's particularly strong in math and the sciences, wouldn't you say, Gabe?"

"Mmm," Gabe assented.

"Are you planning to study engineering or something like that in college?" Dad asked.

"I'll probably follow my father into the insurance business," Bryan said, "so more likely than not I'll major in business."

"Bryan's dad is on the board of directors of Vanguard Fire and Casualty," Gabe put in, reaching for his cocoa cup.

I could tell Mom and Dad were pleased with Bryan, but I found the whole thing excruciating. You would think he was being interviewed for the job of son-in-law the way they were grilling him. I hadn't gotten to be sixteen, though, without finding out what was negotiable in my family and what wasn't. I knew Mom and Dad would think they were failing in their duty as parents if they didn't cross-examine every boy who took me out.

"What about you, Gabe?" Mom asked politely. "Have you given any thought to college yet?"

"Not really," he said. "I thought after school I might strike out on my own as a soldier of fortune."

"A soldier of fortune?" Mom said blankly.

"The navy is a good career for a young man who wants adventure," Dad said.

Gabe shook his head. "Not for me, I'm afraid," he said. "I don't like to shine my shoes and I don't like to take orders." He regarded the battered toe of his shoe thoughtfully.

I was just as glad Gabe wasn't the subject of this interview because he was not giving the right answers. Bryan, however, kept on steadily plugging away at projecting the image of a boy who was honest, hard-working, trustworthy, and brave. "Last month they had college day at school," he put in quickly, "and that was really interesting. Representatives of different colleges came to talk to us informally so we could get an idea of what they had to offer. What I'm looking for, I think, is a really balanced program. I don't want to narrow my choices too soon."

Dad beamed approvingly. I began to think Bryan must really like me, or he would never be going to so much trouble to impress my folks.

Finally the boys were released from the inquisition and allowed to go home. After they left, I went in and collapsed on the bed in my room. Why, I thought, couldn't I reorganize my mind along more useful lines? All I needed to do was to be humble toward Miss May, forget all about Mike and Mimsy, see Gabe as a friend, and fall for Bryan the way he was clearly falling for me. I punched my pillow hard.

Instead, I was doing just the opposite of what I should. I burned with hatred toward Miss May, felt humiliated by Mike and Mimsy, had fallen for Gabe in a big way, and saw Bryan only as a friend. Weren't things ever going to get easy?

Chapter Five

Monday Miss May handed out individual type-written pages to each person in the English class listing guidelines for the reports we were supposed to do on English novelists. Mine was on Charles Dickens and had a long list of things to be covered in the report, like "Dickens's early life" and "social conditions in Victorian England." Small subject, that! I thought. At the bottom of the page was a list of questions that should be answered in the report—date of birth, works published, and so on. Miss May didn't believe in giving people a free hand.

I've got to be careful not to lose this, I thought. I realized that the sheet was irreplaceable. If I lost it, there wasn't going to be anything I could do except go to Miss May and confess, and face her full wrath and ridicule. In fact, the smart thing to do would be to go uptown this very afternoon, photocopy ten copies of it, and put one in a vault somewhere.

"Does everyone have his or her instruction sheet?" asked Miss May. "I haven't overlooked anyone? Very well. We will not be having our regular class today because instead you will all go to the art room to meet the political cartoonist, Charles Minchin. The administration seems to feel this is more important than the development of the novel. I am instructed to ask that you each bring paper and a pencil."

I got so excited I dropped my pencil. It hit the floor and its point snapped off.

"Take your books with you," Miss May said. "This activity will consume the remainder of the period."

Everyone jumped up and headed out the door. I grabbed my books and forced my way across the room to the pencil sharpener. Why did I have to break my dumb pencil? Now I would get behind and I'd probably get a rotten seat, and this was something I was really interested in.

I sharpened my pencil with a whir and a flurry of wood shavings, then headed out the door with everybody else in a stampede to the art room. Mr. Minchin was sitting on a table, a lanky man who looked as if he had been carelessly strung together with shoelaces. The minute I saw him I liked him. He had big ears, a long humorous mouth, and his hair was falling in his eyes. Luckily, I was able to get a good place to sit after all. I was really excited. I love cartoons. This was the kind of enrichment and cultural opportunity I could go for.

"I'm Charles Minchin," he said. "You can call me Charlie. Now, everybody got a pencil? I'm going to give you a few pointers on the art of caricature. Do you kids know what a caricature is?" He looked at us dubiously.

"Yes, sir," said Eliot Sanders.

Mr. Minchin winced. "Don't call me sir, kid. I'm not that old yet. Now in a caricature, you want to make somebody look just like themselves, only more so, if you get me." He picked up a piece of chalk. "Take my pal Stan Morrison, your headmaster." He sketched a curved line on the board with a squiggle at the end, did a little dip under that for the chin, threw a few more dashes in and drew in the hairline. It was really amazing. It was Mr. Morrison to the life.

We all laughed and there was a scattering of applause.

"Nothing to it," he said. He pointed to the squiggle. "Now, you see, Stan is a good-looking, sweet-looking sort of fellow. He doesn't have a big beak of a nose and monstrous Adam's apple like lots of guys do, so what you notice about Stan is the absence of the nose, if you see what I mean."

I personally had never noticed Mr. Morrison's nose one way or another, but I was breathless with interest.

He waved his hand over the upper part of the drawing. "Here you see the broad, bland forehead of honest Stan, only broader and blander and the smooth hair we make into a bathing cap." He grinned. "Now does everybody have a pencil?"

We all nodded. What I was dying to caricature was Charles Minchin himself. Piece of cake, I thought, with those big ears and that floppy hair.

"You don't get to do me," he said, crushing my hopes at once. "I want you to pick out the boy that's nearest to you and do him."

"We don't do girls?" said Christie. "Only boys?"

"That's right," said Mr. Minchin. "In my long and misspent life I've found it safest never to do women and girls. Skip doing them, and I promise you, you'll live a lot longer."

I thought that was a pretty sexist thing to say, but on the other hand I was just as relieved that nobody was going to be searching my face for funny-looking features.

Gabe was the boy closest to me, but due, no doubt, to a certain emotional involvement, I didn't see anything funny about Gabe's face at all, so I did Eliot. I had to make several tries at it before I got him, but finally I was pleased enough to stop and put my initials in the corner of the drawing.

I looked around and saw that everybody else was still breathing hard over their papers, so I sneaked out another piece of paper and did a quick drawing of Charles Minchin. He was too good to pass up.

He must have caught me looking at him because he strolled over to my table and looked at my sketch. I deftly slid the drawing I'd done of him under the drawing of Eliot before he reached me.

"Very nice," he said. "I recognize our young friend over there. Do you think we should show it to him?"

I wasn't sure, but Eliot leaned over and looked at it anyway. "That doesn't look a bit like me," he said scornfully.

"It's a principle of caricature," said Mr. Minchin, "that nobody ever recognizes themselves. Nevertheless, let me assure you that the little lady has a lot of talent. Now, what do we have here?" He pulled the hidden sheet out and, as I blushed, looked at the sketch I had done of him.

He looked at me. "I see you couldn't resist doing me," he said.

I blushed some more. "You were too good to pass up," I admitted.

"Have you done a lot of drawing?"

"I doodle a lot."

"A natural talent," he said. "Now let me see what the rest of you have here," he said, going around the room.

After the first trial run, he took us slowly over some easier things. He brought out pictures of public figures that we'd all seen caricatures of and did sample ears and noses on the board, demonstrating ways of exaggerating them.

The bell rang, finally, but I was in no hurry to leave. I was having fun. He put the chalk down. "In the end," he said, "it's an art. There are no rules. It's instinct. What you want to do is to find what makes a person recognizable and make it funny."

We all got up to go, and as I passed him he blew me a kiss. "So long, beautiful," he said.

I blushed. I had never spent so much time blushing in my life, but as far as I was concerned it had been a fantastic hour. I was beginning to think that Dad was right about the value of all the cultural enrichment at the academy. After this my doodles were going to be so much richer and more meaningful. Mr. Minchin had opened whole new horizons for me. I guess I had always looked at people with the eye of a cartoonist but without really realizing it.

"Let me see yours," said Gabe when we got out in the hall.

I pulled mine out.

"That looks like old El, all right," he said.

"Now let me see yours," I said.

He grinned. "I don't have the gift," he said. "I'd better get on to my next class before you make me show you my miserable efforts." His books slipped and a paper fluttered down. "Uh-oh," he said, grabbing it. "It's as much as my life is worth to lose that dumb sheet from Miss May's class."

As Gabe charged off down the hall I suddenly had a cold feeling in the pit of my stomach. My instruction sheet from Miss May's class! What had I done with it? My recollection was a bit foggy. When Miss May mentioned the caricature session, the necessity of holding onto that sheet at all costs had temporarily flown out of my mind in all the excitement. Everyone around me was hurrying to the next class, but I stopped where I was and went through all my books and papers. There was no sign of it. My hand began to tremble a little. What could have happened to the thing? Could it have slipped out of my books the way Gabe's had? The problem was that since each person in the class was doing a different author, it would do me no good to get a copy of someone else's instruction sheet. Whatever it took, I had to find mine.

Just then the bell rang and I had to make a run for Spanish class. I felt a little sick. The paper couldn't be gone. It just couldn't be. I would retrace my steps after school, and then sneak into Miss May's room and search. I had to find it.

After school, I sifted through all my books and papers for the sixth time, hoping against hope that I had somehow missed it the first time around, then I began to retrace my path through the halls, looking everywhere. Finally, I came back to Miss May's room. She was just leaving. I saw her close the door behind her and totter off down the hall on her ridiculous strappy heels. I waited until she turned a corner and was out of sight. Then I rushed up to try the door. To my relief the knob turned easily in my hand. I ran to my desk. There was no sign of it there. I probed the metal cubbyhole of the desk with my fingers. I even got down on my knees and looked under it, but all I got for my trouble was grubby knees.

I looked desperately around the room. It had to be here somewhere, I told myself. But I knew too well that it could have been dropped in the halls and carried along on somebody's shoe. It could have floated out a window. Maybe (shudder) somebody had even picked it up and thrown it into the incinerator. Don't panic, I told myself. First search the room completely.

I remembered that I had sharpened my pencil, so I checked around the pencil sharpener. There was no sign of it, but then I slid the filing cabinet next to the sharpener away from the wall and there it was! My paper! It was leaning against the baseboard. I felt like kissing it. But as I picked it up I noticed something strange. The heavy curtain of the window moved and I saw something shiny was behind it. I was curious enough to lift the curtain up and take a peek. To my astonishment there was a bottle of whiskey sitting there.

I picked up my paper, then looked around nervously, and quickly moved the filing cabinet back in place. With the cabinet back against the wall, the edge of the curtain was once more pinned to the wall and the bottle was hidden, but now that I knew it was there in my imagination, it seemed almost to pulsate and glow, like a creature in a science fiction film. The first mad thought that occurred to me was that this was some plot of Miss May's to frame me. I half expected her to walk in surrounded by school officials and shout "Aha!"

I couldn't wait to get out of there. I tucked my important paper into my chemistry book and scooted out of the room. I paused a second in the hall to nervously check and make sure the typed instruction sheet was still safely tucked in my chemistry book, then I fled the building. In spite of my unease about the whiskey bottle, a tremendous wash of relief swept over me now that I had found the missing paper. I hated to think of what would have happened if I hadn't found it. I was positive Miss May was just waiting for the chance to pounce on me if I slipped up in the slightest way. What a lucky thing I'd been able to find it.

As I came out of the building I heard Gabe calling to me. I stopped to wait up for him as he strode toward me, the sun on his hair catching its blond highlights. I liked to watch him walk. I liked everything about him. There was nobody in the world I would rather have run into, and for a crazy second I even let myself hope that he had been watching for me and had waited for me.

"Missed your ride again?" he said.

"That's right. If I'm not there the minute he comes, Blake takes off without me. You'd think the place was a pit stop on a racetrack. I think he doesn't want people to see us together. He's afraid they'll figure out we're related. Blake's kind of weird that way."

"I like Blake," said Gabe.

"You *like* Blake?" I couldn't keep the note of surprise out of my voice.

"Yeah. He's a nice guy."

It was an interesting moment for me. It was the first time it had occurred to me that Blake might have a different side than the one I usually saw.

"Maybe he's just afraid people are going to compare you two," Gabe went on. "I'll bet he thinks people are going around saying you got all the brains in the family."

Gabe obviously liked figuring out what made people tick. He had a theory about Miss May, and now it turned out he had a theory about Blake, too. I supposed he could be right about Blake. It was funny, but even though I'd lived with my brother my whole life I'd never thought much about what went on in his mind. If anybody had asked me why he didn't want me around, I'd have said that's just Blake. Nasty. I was jealous of the way nothing seemed to get to him, but it had never occurred to me that he might be jealous of my good grades.

"What held you up today?" asked Gabe.

"I had to go back and look for that instruction sheet Miss May gave us," I said. "I couldn't find mine."

He whistled.

"It's okay," I said. "I finally found it behind the filing cabinet in Miss May's room. It must have slipped back there when I sharpened my pencil."

"Lucky thing you found it."

"I know." I hesitated a minute, then lowered my voice. "I found something else, too. Did you know there was a bottle of whiskey behind the curtains in the class?"

Gabe's black eyebrows shot up.

"No kidding," I said. "A whiskey bottle. At least, I'm pretty sure that's what it was. It looked like a whiskey bottle."

"Must have been, then," said Gabe. "Nothing else looks like a whiskey bottle. I mean, we know it wasn't a flower vase, right?"

"There's probably a perfectly logical explanation," I said. "Maybe Miss May was taking it to a party and forgot it? Or maybe she gargles with it or uses it to sterilize her staples or something like that."

"I have a better idea. Miss May is a secret lush."

"You think so?" I was intrigued by the idea. I had never known anybody who was a secret lush, but my grandmother, past president of the Woman's Christian Temperance Union, had once told me that alcohol turned people into beasts, and I had to admit I'd never known anybody more beastly than Miss May.

"Sure," said Gabe. "When you think about it, that might explain a lot."

"I don't know. I don't think she's drunk in class, do you? I have the idea that drunks bump into tables and fall over things."

"I guess you're right," he agreed. "She can't be drunk in class. It'd be too risky. But what's with the bottle, then?"

"My friend, Mary Jo, who has a weight problem, always stuffs her pocketbook with peanut butter crackers when she goes to something like a concert," I suggested helpfully. "It's because she can't stand the idea she's going to be stuck in there with no way to get to food. The crackers are sort of like a panic button. Maybe it's like that."

"Maybe," said Gabe. "You know, we could sort of keep an eye out. Smell her breath, that sort of thing."

"Not me," I said. "I'm not getting close enough to Miss May to smell her breath. Not if I can help it."

Gabe grinned. "I see what you mean," he said. "Hey, has Bryan called you yet about Saturday night?"

"No," I said. I held my breath and willed him to say that since I was free, maybe I could go out with him Saturday night. He didn't.

"He'll probably call you tonight," he said. "He's got tickets to the symphony in Raleigh."

"Who else is going?" I said. To me my voice sounded far away but I hoped Gabe wouldn't notice.

"I'm taking Christie," he said.

"Not Amelia."

He looked amused. "I never take out the same girl twice in a row. It only encourages them."

I looked steadfastly at the ground. I was feeling awful.

"Bryan's a nice guy, don't you think?" said Gabe.

"Oh, yes," I said faintly.

"I like him," he said.

"I like him, too," I said.

"Well, that's good, because he sure likes you."

This was the most awful conversation I had ever had in my life. "He's a very warm person," I said desperately. "I can tell he'd be a good friend."

Friendship was definitely the theme I wished to develop, and I was pleased I had somehow managed to work the word "friend" in.

"Yeah," he said. "He is."

There was a silence. What I should say, I thought, is something about how I didn't believe in settling down with just one boy. But as the seconds ticked by it got more and more awkward to say anything at all.

We had reached Gabe's house and he turned into the driveway. "See you Saturday night," he said.

I stifled a sigh. See you Saturday night. What a lovely sound those words would have had under slightly different circumstances.

I walked the rest of the way home thinking about what a mess my life was. Why didn't Gabe ask me out? Why didn't Miss May drop dead? Above all, why couldn't I just quit caring about either of those things?

Chapter Six

As Gabe had predicted, Bryan called and asked me out for Saturday night. I could have said no, but it wasn't as if I had anything else to do. Besides, Gabe, Bryan, Mom, and Dad all obviously expected me to go to the symphony with Bryan, and going was easier than claiming that Saturday was the evening I always washed my hair.

Saturday evening, though, when I got into the car I immediately had a premonition this was not going to be the fun evening of my life. I could see that Christie had gone to a lot of trouble to get dressed for her date with Gabe. She was actually, unless I was hallucinating, wearing two colors of mascara, blue from the roots of the lashes out, and black at the tips. Furthermore, something had happened to her soft, fluffy hair. It had been stiffened and swirled until she looked like a country and western singer.

"Hi, there, Tish!" she squealed. "Isn't it a gorgeous evening?"

Since it was thirty-seven degrees and starting to rain, I was at a loss for what to say. I immediately sensed that Christie was not at her most relaxed. There was nothing for me to do, though, but to slide in next to Bryan and brace myself. It looked as if it was going to be a grim evening.

"You're cold," Bryan said, leaning toward me as I took his hand. His smoky voice managed to make my cold hands sound like a special secret between the two of us.

Gabe turned on the ignition and headed the car out toward Raleigh, its headlights bouncing against the rain.

"I just love symphonies," Christie said quickly, her voice sounding strained. "My very favorite thing in the world is an evening of music. Ever since I was little I've had this special feeling for music. I liked to listen to the ringing of the ice cream truck, things like that. I think music really touches a person deeply, if you see what I mean."

"Uh, sure," said Gabe. He shot her a puzzled glance, doubtless trying to account for the hysterical note in her voice. He evidently did not suspect, as I did, that a desire to please him was responsible.

"Schubert," she said desperately, "I just love Schubert and his 'Song Without Words.' Or was that Liszt? Could I mean Mendelssohn? Anyway, it's just beautiful. I could just listen to it all night. And Bach, those Brandenburg Concerti—dum, dum-dum, dum dum. Just like a merry-go-round. Positively scrumptious, that's all. And as for Beethoven, I'm just crazy about Beethoven.''

She was talking faster and faster.

Meanwhile, in the back seat, Bryan closed both of his big hands over mine, possessively. "What matters," he murmured softly in my ear, "is who you're listening to Beethoven with."

I swallowed hard, stifling the impulse to say "Down, boy, down."

"If I ever get caught up in Chemistry," I said flatly, "I'm going to try out for the chamber music ensemble." I was determined to turn the conversation into neutral channels.

"I'll bet you play well," said Christie wistfully.

"I guess I'm not too bad," I said, suddenly embarrassed.

Bryan put his arm around me and squeezed. "You practice every day, I'll bet."

"I suppose I do," I admitted. Actually, I thought everybody did. How else could you learn the pieces?

"I had a feeling you did," said Bryan. "My instincts tell me you're one of those good kids who always does what they're supposed to do."

I couldn't think why it should be so irritating to be called a good kid. The fact was, I did try hard to do what I was supposed to do. So why when he said that, was I suddenly overcome with a vision of myself dancing a wild fandango as I held a knife in my teeth. "Aha, gringo," I said in my fantasy. "So you theenk I am a good gur-rel. Take that! And that!" I flung a rose at my feet and stomped on it. "Estrellita does not take such insults!"

"A penny for your thoughts," said Bryan.

"I wasn't thinking about anything in particular," I said quickly. If Bryan kept asking me about what was on my mind, some day he was going to get an awful shock. I had some very flaky thoughts.

As it turned out the symphony that night was better than the movie in one respect—I didn't have to give a running commentary to Bryan about it. It was worse in another respect, though. There was an hour's drive home afterward in which Bryan could nuzzle me in the back seat.

"Come a little closer," he whispered in my ear.

"I have to stay in my seat belt," I said.

"You know," he said, "the next time we're going to have to bring Belle along. She's starting to feel left out."

I did not for a minute think that Bryan's dog, Belle, was sitting home pining because she had missed a symphony. I knew what was on Bryan's mind. He wanted to bring Belle along so he could walk me up to the door without Gabe and have a private good night kiss, that was what. I was starting to feel sort of trapped. Bryan was a difficult person to rebuff. He sort of ignored all hints and enveloped you in warmth.

We dropped Christie off at her house in High Acres subdivision. By then she had been bubbling in Gabe's direction for an hour with no visible results, and his calm politeness had obviously hurt her. I felt a little sad to see that as they walked toward the house her step had completely lost its bounce. For that matter, I wasn't feeling too great myself. It had been a rough evening.

After we let Christie off, we drove to my house, and Gabe and Bryan walked me up to the door. The drizzle was falling steadily now. Rain settled in fine droplets on my hair and dropped down the back of my neck. By the time my hand was on the knob of the front door, my hair was sticking to my face in damp ringlets. It didn't seem to matter. Bryan couldn't see it, and Gabe obviously didn't care what my hair looked like.

"It was a lovely evening," I said, turning toward them both.

In the light from the porch lamp I could see that Gabe's hair was dark with rain and his eyebrows glistened. Bryan was pretty wet, too. He wiped some beads of water off his tough-looking face with one hand and said, "The weather is not the greatest."

"Can't have everything," I said, my teeth chattering. Then in spite of myself I giggled. I had started to see the funny side of it all. How could I have got myself in a position where I had to watch the boy of my dreams being vamped by every girl in school while his friend breathed heavily all over me in the back seat? I seemed to have this unfailing instinct for self-destruction. First Mike, who promptly threw me over for Mimsy, and now this. On top of it all, I had to stand here in the rain saying I'd had a good time. It was so awful, it was funny.

Suddenly Mom and Dad swung the dront door open, and the bright light from the house made the falling raindrips into a halo of diamonds. "Come in, you kids," Mom said. "You must be freezing. What ghastly weather. Let's get you some hot tea."

I stepped quickly inside out of the rain and shook the wetness out of my hair like a dog. I was past caring about glamor. All I wanted was warm ears.

My first primitive emotion was delight at being inside where it was warm, but on deeper consideration I decided I didn't like the way things were shaping up. It was not standard for Mom and Dad to ask my dates to come in two times running. Their usual habit was a thorough going-over of the guy on the first date and only spot checks thereafter to make sure he hadn't suddenly sprouted fangs. I didn't like this business of inviting Bryan in a second time. Of course, maybe they had asked Bryan and Gabe in just because the weather was so awful—but what if that wasn't the reason? What if Bryan had overdone the business of impressing them and they liked him so much they wanted to make friends with him? If they started asking him over for dinner and things like that, he was going to think they were doing it because I was crazy about him. Pretty soon he was going to start feeling almost like a member of the family. A chill shot through me that had nothing to do with my dripping hair.

Dad went in to click off the television in the family room while Mom went to get the teapot. "We've been watching a special report on the Middle East," Dad explained, wheeling himself into the living room.

"I'm sorry I had to miss that," Bryan said. "I wanted to see what slant they were going to take. It was too bad they had to run it on the same night as the symphony."

"I think it was a pretty balanced report," Dad said, as we followed him into the living room.

The three of us, Gabe, me, and Bryan, got settled on the couch. Symbolically enough, I was in the middle. Immediately, Dad and Bryan plunged into a full hashing out of the situation in the Middle East. Both of them were so appallingly well-informed that it looked as if it could go on all night. Gabe and I propped our weary selves up with couch pillows and did our best to look awake. Mom poured out a cup of tea for Bryan and handed it to him, beaming. She loves for young people to be serious-minded and interested in current events. I noticed Gabe was looking into his cup with an expression suggesting he only wished it contained cyanide, and I sympathized.

I yawned broadly. I couldn't stand it any longer. "I think I'd better call it an evening," I said. "I'm awfully tired."

"I'd better be going, too," said Gabe quickly. "I've got to get up in the morning."

"Gabe's always hitting the books," said Bryan. "He spends every Saturday morning slogging away at the library."

"Anything to get out of the house," Gabe said, looking a bit annoyed.

I presumed he didn't like to be called hard-working any more than I had liked being called good. It occured to me that if Bryan could have caught the expression on people's faces, he'd have figured out by now that nobody wanted the drudge of the year award. People like to think others saw them as effortlessly brilliant, even if they do put in long hard hours of work.

The two boys went out into the drizzle, Bryan with a hand on Gabe's arm, and Mom closed the door behind them. She said, "Bryan is such an outstanding young man, don't you think?"

I yawned noncommittally.

"I think it would be fun to have him over to dinner sometime," said Mom, "so we could get to know him better. Wouldn't that be nice?"

"You and Dad don't have to fall all over yourselves being nice to Bryan just for me," I said.

"But we like Bryan," Mom said.

"But if you keep on being extra nice to him," I said, "he's going to think that *I* like him."

"Well, don't you?"

"Sure, I like him, but I don't *like* him, if you know what I mean."

Mom smiled at me. "I think I see what you mean," she said. "These things can't be rushed. Your father and I won't push things. I can't help being impressed with Bryan though. He seems to manage his life so capably in spite of his handicap. And he seems so solid and reliable. He really is a remarkable person."

This conversation was beginning to remind me of the morning I overslept and woke up to find my transfer to the academy had been completely arranged. I knew Mom and Dad were gung ho on equal rights for the handicapped, but I didn't want my dating Bryan to be a part of their personal affirmative action program. My love life had enough problems without its being a cause.

I understood Mom's point of view. I sort of admired Bryan's coolness under pressure myself. I knew things weren't easy for him. But even though I liked Bryan, I couldn't imagine I would ever have anything to say to him that couldn't be said over a loudspeaker in a football stadium.

Keep calm, I told myself. This is not the Middle Ages. There are no such things as arranged marriages anymore.

That night I dreamed that Gabe and I were having a picnic.

"Have some Cracker Jacks," he said, holding out the box to me. "I love you. I adore you."

"I know you adore me," I said, "but as a world-famous cartoonist, I have an obligation to my public."

"I'll wait for you," he said.

At that point I heard the flapping wings of a large bird and looked up to see an enormous crow with the face of Miss May. She looked a lot like the illustration of a harpy in my tenth-grade Latin book.

"I think you'd better hold on tight to those Cracker Jacks," I said calmly. "That bird might steal the free prize which is included in each package."

With great presence of mind, Gabe sat on the Cracker Jacks. As Miss May flew on, he looked at me admiringly. "You are so wise," he said.

"I know," I said. "People are always telling me that."

The next morning I slept late and woke up, under the spell of the dream, feeling that I could straighten out my life if I just worked hard enough on it.

Unfortunately, promptly on Monday Miss May sent home progress reports and reality crashed down on me. I realized there were things about my life that were going to be impossible to straighten out, and one of them was Miss May.

When I got home from school I threw the report on the kitchen table. Mom was kneading bread and her fingers were all covered with flour, but she came over and looked at it. "What is it?" she said.

"It's a progress rport," I growled.

Westover Academy prided itself on frequent progress reports to keep parents informed. Maybe the idea was sound, but seeing my only grade in English so far listed as "Grade average = 0" did nothing to cheer me up.

"It does look bad," Mom said in soothing tones, "but you told me yourself you'll get to drop that lowest grade."

"But look at the comment!" I said.

Mom turned her eyes toward the comment written in Miss May's spiky handwriting—"Letitia seems to believe that her gifts excuse carelessness in her everyday work."

"I could kill that woman," I said. "I could kill her cheerfully before breakfast and cook her on the griddle and feed her to the cats, except that they probably wouldn't eat her because they are so fussy, and then I would take the leftovers and put them in the garbage disposal and give her ugly clothes to the Salvation Army and the world would be a better place."

"Letitia!" said Mom in shocked tones.

I immediately felt ashamed. "She just makes me so mad," I said.

Mom went back to kneading her bread. "She doesn't seem to have the right touch with young people," Mom said. "She probably doesn't realize how much we all need encouragement. I wouldn't be surprised if underneath she is very unhappy person. We should try to feel compassion for her."

I tried to feel compassion for Miss May and failed.

Mom flipped over the bread and plunged her fists into its doughy mass. "We don't want to fall into the trap of being unkind," she said. "As your grandmother always says, 'Kind hearts are more than coronets.'"

I thought it was a shame Grandmother had never met Miss May. Maybe then she'd have come up with a quotation that was more to the point, like "Praise the Lord and pass the ammunition."

"Why don't you help yourself to an orange," Mom said. "Aunt Ellen shipped us some beautiful ones from Florida."

Mom seemed to think that all a person needed to smooth their path in life was something to nibble on.

"I'm not hungry," I said.

In the mood I was in, the last thing I wanted to do was to go to the library and work on my report on Dickens. But the more Miss May was obviously out to get me, the more important it was that my work be absolutely beyond reproach so as not to give her a toehold. So as soon as the steam quit coming out of my ears, I hoisted my books on my hip and headed toward the back door. "I need to go to the library to work on my Dickens report," I told Mom. "Is it all right if I have the car?"

"Of course," she said. "I like to see you taking a constructive approach to your problems, Tish. That's my good girl."

I drove to the library thinking murderous thoughts. What Mom didn't seem to realize was that I was not as nice as she and Dad were. I could get mad. Really, really mad. And the person who could unfailingly make me mad was Miss May. I didn't see why she had to be out to get me when I was trying so hard to do what I was supposed to do! It wasn't fair.

I hoped studying at the library would help calm me down. Not only was the library quiet, but even more important, it was full of first-rate subjects for caricature. There was Mr. Chang at the reference desk with his inscrutable almond eyes and the carnation in his buttonhole. Sometimes a tramp with hair growing out of his ears and a red nose would be dozing among the magazines. Or there might be a middle-aged woman with a figure like a pouter pigeon browsing among the historical novels. I promised myself the treat of a half hour drawing the people in the library after I finished working on my Dickens report. Maybe that would cheer me up.

Ever since Mr. Minchin had given his little workshop for us, I had started doing caricatures all the time. My favorite subject, of course, was Miss May with a python around her neck. But I wasn't particular. I would draw anybody who would sit still long enough.

"My daughter the cartoonist," I murmured to myself as I drove toward the library. Maybe it didn't have quite the dignity of "my daughter the doctor" or "my daughter the lawyer," but it sounded like fun.

I wished that while I had had Mr. Minchin around I had asked him what the average salary was for a political cartoonist and whether the job had any fringe benefits or paid vacation. I also would have liked to know whether it was absolutely necessary for the ambitious young political cartoonist to fully understand the Middle East situation.

When I got to the library I immediately looked around to see if some good subjects were there. There was a harassed mother with three kids over by the New Books shelf, but the trouble with young mothers was that they didn't stand still long enough for me to have a chance to draw them. To judge by the way the littlest kid was screaming, the mother would probably be gone before I even finished reading about life in Victorian times. I looked around hopefully for the derelict with the hair in his ears, then suddenly I saw someone who was even more interesting. It was Gabe, over by the card catalog. Forgetting all about caricatures and forgetting about Miss May and Charles Dickens, for that matter, I headed straight for the card catalog.

"Gabe," I whispered. "What are you doing here?"

"Researching F. Scott Fitzgerald and the Roaring Twenties," he said, propping his place in the card catalog open with a pencil. "What about you?"

"Charles Dickens and Victorian times," I said. I found myself noticing how charmingly his hair grew at his temples, soft and sort of combed back. I liked the curve of his jaw, too, and his slightly pink ears. I was in a bad way, all right. When you start getting sentimental about a boy's ears you're pretty much beyond hope.

"How far have you gotten with yours?" he said.

"I've got most of it done," I said. "Just the Victorian part yet to go."

He took my spiral-bound notebook from me and leafed through it. "Hey, this is good, Tish, really good."

I craned my neck. "You think so?" I said doubtfully. I couldn't see anything very exciting about Dickens's place of birth and education.

"I mean the drawings."

I had filled the margins of my notes with caricatures, and I had to admit they were more interesting than Dickens's early life. I blushed. "I get a kick out of doing them," I said.

He turned the notebook at an angle to get a better view. "Now," he said, "who is this lady with the python around her neck?"

"It's Miss May!" we said simultaneously. Then we laughed and Mr. Chang looked daggers at us.

"Who is this fellow with the whiskers and the high collar?" Gabe whispered.

"Dickens, of course."

He turned the page and caught sight of a sinister Oriental with a carnation the size of a sunflower. He mouthed the words "Mr. Chang" and I nodded.

"They all look pretty silly," he murmured. "I hope you aren't going to get it into your head to do one of me."

I looked at him and could sort of feel myself melting like cheese on a grill and getting all gooey. "Oh, no," I said. "I wouldn't do that."

Gabe looked studiously down at my notebook. "You ought to do some for the school paper," he said gruffly. "I know they're looking for something special for the Christmas edition."

I already felt terrible about getting all gooey. How bored Gabe must be at girls getting all gooey. I tried my best to sound brisk. "That's an idea," I said. "Maybe I'll do that."

Just then the front door of the library opened, letting in a blast of cold air that wafted itself over to us at the card catalog. When I felt the cold draft on the back of my neck, I turned around and saw Bryan coming in with his dog, Belle.

I felt myself freeze, as if a flashbulb had caught me in the act of doing something illegal or immoral or fattening. Which was silly because I had every reason in the world to be at the library doing research on Charles Dickens.

I glanced at Gabe and saw he looked positively pale. Suddenly I decided I would like to disappear.

Bryan and Belle had headed over toward the record collection, and I saw I could get out without going right past them, so I just gathered my things together and got out of there.

When I got out to the car I was panting. Why did I feel so guilty? It was not, for Pete's sake, as if I were married to Bryan. I groaned a little and pounded on the steering wheel to relieve my feelings. Then I drove on home.

"Back so soon?" said Mom, looking up as I walked in.

"That's right," I said glumly. "I decided to come home and work on something else."

I went into my room, got a big sheet of blank paper, spread it out on my desk and began to draw. I knew that would put me in a better frame of mind. Just the way that making up a jingle about Miss May had kept me from going crazy that time she gave me a zero, making a great big bunch of caricatures would help me keep my sense of perspective. Maybe the wrong boy was interested in me, but I knew at least that what I drew for myself on that white sheet of paper would be just the way I wanted it.

I drew a big Christmas party for the teachers, complete with a dinky Christmas tree on top of a filing cabinet. Mr. Morrison, with a skimpy white beard that did not hide his dimples, was dressed as Santa Claus. Then I added a sketch of Miss May sitting on a bookcase with her shoes falling off. She was holding a bottle which I carefully labeled ginger ale, and she looked as full of Christmas cheer as Scrooge. Next I put Mr. Alonzo, the janitor, at the door with holly twined around his broom. Before long I was lost in the drawing and my problems seemed far away. I kept drawing and drawing until the paper was filled and the Christmas party was a madhouse, with teachers in every available space, their party hats askew and holly pinned to their lapels. It took me quite a while. Finally I polished it off with a black cat on the desk, his paws over his eyes to shut out all the confusion. The cat sort of represented me, I guess, trying to block out my troubles.

I breathed a sigh of satisfaction. There it was, my own world, with everybody sitting just where I had put them and doing just what I said. I put a few finishing touches on Mr. Alonzo's mustache and re-shaped Mr. Stokes's shoes. It really was good, I thought to myself. Of course, I'd been practicing caricaturing all these people when I'd seen them around school, so it wasn't as if I had done the cartoon completely cold, but it was amazing how nicely it had all taken shape. On an impulse, I picked up the drawing carefully by its corners and carried it down the hall to Blake's room.

As usual a sticker plastered across his door carried the welcoming legend, "Buzz off, buster." I knocked.

A growl came from within.

"I want to show you something," I said.

The door opened and Blake stood at it, blocking the entrance. "Yeah?"

I held up my drawing. I wanted an impartial critic, and I knew that in my house I didn't have far to go to find one. Mom or Dad might be tactful, but I

First
Class
Romance

Delivered to your door by

First Love from Silhouette®

(See inside for special 4 FREE book offer)

Find romance at your door with 4 FREE First Love from Silhouette novels!

Falling in love for the very first time... what's it *really* like? It's easy to find out just how many ways love's magic comes to a girl like you, when you have First Love from Silhouette novels sent right to your home.

This is a special series written just for you, as you discover how warm, how special and how radiant romance can be. You can even receive these tender stories each month to read at home. All you have to do is fill out and mail back the attached postage-paid order card, and you'll get 4 new First Love from Silhouette novels absolutely FREE! It's a $7.80 value... plus we'll send you a FREE Mystery Gift. And there's another bonus: our monthly First Love from Silhouette Newsletter, free with your subscription.

After you receive your free books, you'll have the chance to preview 4 more First Love from Silhouette novels for 15 days. If you decide to keep them, you'll pay just $7.80— with no extra charge for home delivery and at no risk! You'll also have the option of cancelling at any time. Just drop us a note. Your first 4 books and the Mystery Gift are yours to keep in any case.

First Love from Silhouette®

A FREE
Mystery Gift
awaits you, too!

FILL OUT THIS POSTPAID CARD AND MAIL TODAY!

Mail this card today for your

4 FREE BOOKS
(a $7.80 value) and
a Mystery Gift FREE!

First Love from Silhouette®

Silhouette Books, 120 Brighton Rd., P.O. Box 5084, Clifton, NJ 07015-9956

☐ Yes, please send 4 new First Love from Silhouette novels and Mystery Gift to my home FREE and without obligation. Unless you hear from me after I receive my 4 FREE books, please send me 4 new First Love from Silhouette novels for a free 15-day examination each month as soon as they are published. I understand that you will bill me a total of just **$7.80** with no additional charges of any kind. There is no minimum number of books that I must buy, and I can cancel at any time. No matter what I decide, the first 4 books and the Mystery Gift are mine to keep.

NAME _____
(please print)

ADDRESS _____

CITY _____ STATE _____ ZIP _____

Terms and prices subject to change.
Your enrollment is subject to acceptance by Silhouette Books.

CT7755

could count on Blake telling me what he really thought.

He backed away, then took it from me and carried it over to a window. Amazingly he managed to do this without tripping over the skates and skis and basketballs that covered his floor. "Well, what do you know!" he said. "It's a Christmas party."

"Do you recognize anybody?" I said.

"Sure," he said. "Here's old Alonzo, and that there is the Chemistry teacher, what's-his-name, and...yeah, sure, I recognize lots of people." He looked at me. "Hey, Tish, it's not bad, you know. It's not a bit bad."

I was overwhelmed by such generous praise. "I thought I'd polish it up some and turn it in to the school newspaper," I said.

"I guess there's no chance you're going to enter it anonymously," he said, suddenly glum.

"Of course not," I said. "I want people to know who did it. I want fame and honor in my own time."

"I was afraid of that," he said.

I moved some books off a chair and sat down. "Blake," I said, "I want to ask your opinion about something."

He looked so surprised I thought he might accidentally scrunch the drawing, and I was relieved when he laid it carefully on top of the jeans, socks and old sweatshirts that were on his bed.

"Shoot," he said.

"Do you think Gabe Farrar is ever going to ask me out?"

"Not a chance," he said promptly.

I felt slightly sick because I had the feeling he was right.

"See," he said, "Gabe can have any girl in the school. It's a well-known fact. All he has to do is smile at them, and they just sort of melt in a puddle at his feet. Who can explain it? There's no accounting for girls. But you can see he'd feel like some kind of crumb to cut out Bryan from the only girl Bryan wants."

"Me," I said starkly.

"Yeah, you."

"How could I be so lucky?" I said. "But what if I just quit going out with Bryan?"

He shook his head. "Wouldn't make any difference."

"I don't see why. It seems to me then I'd be a free agent, like in baseball. I'll just quit seeing Bryan."

"Look at it this way," said Blake. "How would you feel about it if Stephanie took up with your old boyfriend, Mike?"

I saw right away what he meant. It might be all over between Mike and me, but by the time I was indifferent enough to Mike to want Stephanie to go out with him, they'd both be gray-haired old pensioners collecting Social Security.

I picked up my drawing off the heap of junk on the bed. "That's all right," I said stoutly. "I will seek fame and fortune as a cartoonist. I will follow my star, lose myself in my work, become hugely successful, and the envy of all. Who cares if Gabe ever asks me out?''

"Good luck," said Blake. I had the awful feeling he was looking at me with pity.

Chapter Seven

Stephanie was quick to offer me advice on my problems, but unfortunately none of it was any good.

"Transfer back to Senior High," she said. "I really miss you. I can't tell you how much. Now I've got Spike Busby for my lab partner." Her pug nose quivered anxiously.

"How would transferring help me, Steph?" I said. "I'd still have the same situation, only I'd have to watch Mike drooling all over Mimsy on top of it."

"It would help me," she confided hoarsely. "I can't stand the way that hood looks at me. He just keeps *looking* at me. It's sinister."

The problem was that now that Stephanie and I were going to different schools, we weren't always on the same wavelength. It was hard for her to envision my problems, and it was certainly hard for me to envision hers.

"Mom and Dad wouldn't let me transfer anyway," I said. "They've already paid for the first semester. Besides, I don't want to get away from Gabe. I want to get closer to him."

"Maybe I should ask for police protection," Stephanie brooded.

"I can't believe the boy's that bad, Stephanie," I said in exasperation.

"He's already missing three of his front teeth, he's got a tattoo that says MOM, and he wears a rhinestone earring," she countered.

"Maybe he's in a band or something," I said. I had to face the fact that Stephanie wasn't going to be much help to me with my problems. We were too out of touch with each other's worlds.

Early the next week, though, I did take a couple of productive steps on my own to improve my life. First, I presented a faultless if boring report on Dickens, for which Miss May gave me a grudging A-, and then I turned in my Christmas cartoon to the school paper.

The newspaper staff didn't send me word about whether they wanted it or not, so I was almost as surprised as anybody else to pick up the special Christmas edition of the *Clarion* and see that the top half of the front page was completely taken up by my cartoon. My heart did a butterfly flutter, and I had to find a place to sit down until it steadied. When I had calmed down, I looked at the drawing with satisfaction. I was glad they had printed it up so big, because it had a lot of detail in it that would have been lost if they had shrunk it. I had only printed my initials in one corner, but the editor, who was obviously a person of great vision and discrimination, had scrupulously typed in below it, "Drawing by Tish Summerlin."

Almost right away people started coming up to congratulate me and after home room I found myself in the midst of a bunch of kids saying, "Way to go, Tish!" and "Hey, I didn't know you did things like that!" "It's just a super cartoon, Tish," said Christie breathlessly. "I mean, that's a major talent you've got there. I just giggled myself silly, that's all."

Bryan heard the commotion, and he and his dog, Belle, came over. "Tish!" he said.

I turned towards him, feeling a little sheepish. It was so easy for me to avoid Bryan and so hard for him to track me down that I felt a little guilty I hadn't spoken to him first. "Hi, Bryan," I said.

Kids started moving on to their next class. "I hear you've had a triumph," Bryan said.

"They did put my cartoon in the school paper," I said.

"Everybody thinks it's great," he said.

I immediately felt crummy that Bryan couldn't see the cartoon. There was no way I could think of that he would get anything out of a caricature. Even if he could feel the lines, it probably wouldn't mean much to him. The proportions of people's noses and chins and ears were probably not things that were at all important to him. It was unlikely he would see what was funny about exaggerating them.

I realized I hadn't said anything for a while, so I quickly said, "I guess people do like it. Maybe I'll be famous in my own time."

"I think this calls for a celebration," he said warmly. "Let's go out to a really good restaurant and whoop it up. I'll see if Gabe can dig up somebody for tonight."

Oh, I expect Gabe can dig up somebody for tonight, I thought sourly. Gabe could always dig somebody up. But the last thing in the world I wanted to do was to go out to dinner with Bryan and yet another girl who was trying to impress Gabe. My only problem was I honestly couldn't see how I could say no. Bryan was making such a generous unselfish offer to help me celebrate that I didn't see how I could be petty enough to tell him no.

"That sounds like fun," I said faintly.

"I'll try to get it clear with Gabe and give you a call right after school," he said.

The rest of the day people I didn't even know kept coming up to me to compliment me on the drawing. Miss May was even more frosty than usual, but I didn't think anything of it. I was too busy enjoying my sudden fame to worry about her. In the back of my mind I was dreading a little the business of going out to dinner with Bryan. I knew I needed to cool that relationship off, and going out to dinner with him was not a step in the right direction. But maybe it would turn out that Gabe wasn't free, I thought. Maybe it wouldn't come off.

After English class, Gabe ran to catch up with me in the hall. "So you took my advice," he said, "and sent one into the paper. Honest, Tish, that is one terrific cartoon."

"I owe all my success, ladies and gentlemen," I said, "to Gabe Farrar, who knew I had it in me."

He put an arm around me and squeezed me. "Congratulations," he said.

I could feel my books slipping out of my stunned fingers, and my knees started feeling like jelly.

"Bryan tells me we're going out to celebrate tonight," he said.

That put the stiffening back in my knees. "Yup," I said in a subdued voice.

"I thought maybe a fast food place," said Gabe, "but Bry wants to pull out all the stops." I heard an edge of bitterness come into his voice. I must have shot him a puzzled look because he added, "Bryan is picking up the tab."

"That makes sense," I said, "if he's the one that wants the big bash."

"I guess so," he said, then he turned down the east-west corridor and disappeared.

People were funny, I thought. As far as I was concerned, Gabe had everything. He was smart, he was funny, he was kind, everybody liked him. But he felt bad because he was short of money. Sometimes I wondered if anybody in the world was really happy. I used to think maybe my brother was happy, but lately I'd come to see I was wrong about that.

Everybody had their problems, even old goof-off Blake.

After school Bryan called to confirm our date and said we'd be going to the Chateau.

"The Chateau, the Chateau," I muttered distractedly as I hung up. "Mo-ther!" I wailed.

Mom was a terrific help. She pressed my dress, lent me her pearls, and gave me pointers.

"But it's been so long," I wailed, "since I've been anyplace that I didn't carry my own food to the table and unwrap it. I can't even remember the last time I was at a restaurant that had forks. How will I know the right one to use?"

"It's very simple, really, Tish," Mom said. "You begin with the piece of silverware that's farthest out and slowly work your way in toward the plate. For example, if soup were the first course, there would be a soup spoon at the extreme edge. It's not hard. Just remember that nice people don't notice other people's table manners and be your own sweet self. It's supposed to be fun, darling. Relax."

"It's supposed to be fun," I repeated dully.

It seemed no time until the doorbell rang. I grabbed my coat and opened the door. To my surprise, Bryan was standing at the door alone. No sign of Gabe. Then I saw he had Belle with him. She smiled at me, baring her canines.

"Hi, Bryan," I said, adding nervously, "Hi, Belle. Gee, Belle sure looks...uh, happy."

"She loves eating out," said Bryan.

I took Bryan's arm, and Belle let us both down the path and to the car.

"Do you know Monica, Tish?" Gabe asked, as we slid into the back seat.

"I don't think so," I said.

A girl with an absolutely splendid pair of blue eyes was regarding me from the front seat. "I just loved your cartoon," Monica breathed. "You are so talented. Isn't she, Gabe?"

"Yup," he said, turning on the ignition.

Monica had long, blond hair that was curved around loosely in back into a fashionable roll. She also had long tapering fingers that were resting lightly on the back of Gabe's neck. I detested her instantly.

"Thank you," I managed to say. I tried to get a hold on myself. Be reasonable, I told myself. If that girl didn't have her fingers on the back of Gabe's neck, you might be absolutely crazy about her. She probably has a wonderful warm heart and is kind to small children.

This is it, I told myself. This is absolutely finished, the end, the last time I go out on these crazy awful dates with Bryan and Gabe. I don't know why it hadn't occurred to me that the more I went out with Bryan, the harder it was going to be to break off with him. Now he was going to take me out to the Chateau and spend a fortune on me and then I would feel worse than ever about breaking off with him.

"Have you ever been to the Chateau, Monica?" said Bryan.

"Oh, yes," she cooed. "It's Mummy and Daddy's very favorite restaurant. In fact, Daddy always jokes that they should have made Armand, the headwaiter, my godfather and then they could be sure of always getting a decent table." She smiled, showing perfect teeth.

I could tell that Bryan was a little let down that the Chateau was old hat to Monica. Well, that was okay. I would be impressed enough for two of us.

The Chateau was the sort of restaurant where people went to get engaged or to entertain on their expense account. When we got there I felt edgy just walking up the steps. There turned out to be a positive army of waiters at our table, all dressed in black and hovering at our elbows. And when I opened the menu it was so large that it effectively blocked out my view not only of Gabe and Monica, but of most of the dining room.

"What sort of thing do you think you want?" I said to Bryan, looking at the menu with dismay. Reading it aloud to Bryan would be like launching into *War and Peace*.

"I always have the filet mignon," he said. "Don't worry about me. Just decide on what you'd like."

Filet mignon, I reflected. Wasn't that some sort of steak? That sounded fairly boring. I felt I should take this chance to have something new and different, something I wouldn't be likely to be offered again. Unfortunately, the menu, besides being long, was in French, and I began to get a little dizzy looking at it.

I looked up at the four waiters hovering around us and tried to decide which one was in charge. Finally, I said timidly to all of them, "What would you suggest?"

"Has mademoiselle tried tripes *à la mode de Caen*?" said the waiter who looked like a retired prime minister. "It is the dish of my homeland, wonderful Normandy. Ah, the taste of it brings to one the smell of the apple trees, the sound of the sea..."

"That sounds good," I said with relief, folding the enormous menu. One of the waiters whipped it out of my hand.

"I'll have the lamb *navarin*," said Monica. She had the air of someone who actually knew what was in lamb *navarin*. She smiled at me, and I realized with a sinking of the heart that she was undeniably attractive. Maybe Gabe thought so, too.

"I'll have the filet mignon," said Gabe.

"Make that three filet mignons," said Bryan. "Belle is crazy about steak."

Soon the courses began in a dignified parade of food. I supposed there was some French superstition against having more than one kind of food before you at once because we only got one dish at a time. First I got a little bitty piece of cold salmon in a pastry crust, and the waiter hovered at my elbow ladling some sort of green mayonnaise sauce on the salmon.

"Ees everything satisfactory, mademoiselle?" asked my waiter. I nodded numbly. Then the salmon was whipped away and the omelet was brought on.

"They always have omelets here with the dinners," Bryan told me. "It's a specialty of the house. You don't have to eat it all."

I took his advice and just nibbled at the omelet. I was saving myself for the main course.

Finally the waiter came with the main courses. He deftly served each of us our main dish and was left standing there with the extra filet mignon, looking a little nonplussed.

"That one is for the dog," Gabe explained. There was a muffled growl from under the table. Belle could smell the steak and was not pleased with the delay in getting hers.

"Of course," said the waiter smoothly, kneeling to serve Belle at Bryan's feet.

You had to give those waiters credit. Nothing ruffled them. The only thing was, they simply didn't go away. They stayed at the table, continually hovering at our elbows, which sort of impeded conversation.

"I think it's wonderful," said Monica, lifting a forkful of stewed lamb to her lips, "that we can celebrate Tish's success this way. Where did you ever learn to draw like that, Tish?"

I made modest noises.

"A talent like that," Bryan said, "should be developed. You should take art courses."

"Maybe so," I said. "It's even crossed my mind that someday I might like to be a..." Suddenly, feeling the eyes of the waiters on my neck, I was not sure I could say that I wanted to be a cartoonist. I felt sure that would not measure up to their impeccable standards.

"A what?" said Bryan.

I swallowed. "A cartoonist," I said.

The waiter who looked like a prime minister smiled gaily. I could imagine how they would all chortle together back in the kitchen when they went to collect the dessert. A cartoonist. Ha, ha, how quaint. I realized I hadn't yet tasted my food, so I chose a fork at random from the array beside my plate. The food smelled absolutely out of this world, and had little bits of cooked celery and carrots in the sauce as well as strips of something that looked like leather. I tasted a carrot, then a bit of celery, and finally worked myself up to tasting a strip of the tripe. It tasted exactly like leather. A little tear came to my eye. What a waste to have all that beautiful, wonderful sauce used on leather.

"How's the tripe?" Gabe said, eyeing me keenly.

Feeling the intimidating eyes of the waiters upon me I said, "F-fine. I don't think I've ever had tripe before. It's, uh, interesting."

"What is tripe, anyway?" said Bryan.

I admired him for being willing to ask.

"The stomach of a cow," said Gabe.

My fork slipped out of my hand and clattered against my plate and down to the floor before my horrified gaze. "I will get for mademoiselle another fork," said the waiter at my elbow, producing one as if from his sleeve. I already had lots of forks I wasn't using, but I meekly took the new fork he handed me and prepared to approach the tripe once more. I fortified myself by thinking of the Queen of England touring her dominions. She probably had to eat all kinds of yucky things like sheep's eyes and seaweed and octopus and yet she seeemd to be in the pink of health. So undoubtedly this tripe stuff wouldn't kill me.

After this, I thought, I'll know better than to choose a regional delicacy. I don't know why it hadn't hit me before that I didn't even like the regional dishes of my own region. Grits and gravy, for instance.

Sounds from under the table told me that Belle was enjoying her dinner much more than I was mine.

I seemed to be pecking at the tripe forever, but finally the waiters whipped away the unspeakable stuff and brought on the dessert, a little meringue the size of a quarter. I supposed it would have been the perfect size for somebody who had already stuffed themselves on salmon and omelet and tripe, but from my point of view it looked kind of small. I touched it with my fork and it shattered into twelve pieces, which I tried to chivy up on my fork. I decided I would have a nice peanut butter sandwich when I got home. There were no hidden pitfalls in a peanut butter sandwich.

Finally, the most dignified of the waiters, the one who looked like a king in exile, with touches of gray at his temples and a haughty nose, came with the check on a little tray and laid it down between Gabe and Bryan. I could see it was a very nasty moment for Gabe. "It's the check, Bryan," he said, because the waiter had walked on such little cat feet over the carpeted floor that Bryan had no way of knowing that the check had arrived. Bryan produced a credit card from his wallet and, groping for the check, laid the credit card on top of it. The waiter smiled and vanished like a genie.

I saw that red patches had appeared on Gabe's neck and in front of his ears and his lips had a white, pinched look. He really did not like for Bryan to have to pick up the check.

"It was a marvelous dinner, Bryan," Monica said. "I have such a weakness for lamb, I could eat it every night."

"Now we all have to go home and diet," said Bryan amiably. I was not sure if Bryan and Monica realized how much Gabe did not like Bryan's picking up the check, but I felt Gabe's tension as if it were a violin string under my fingers.

On the ride home, Gabe was rather silent.

"So what did you think of the Chateau, Tish?" asked Bryan.

"I have never been in such a fancy restaurant," I said.

"And what did you think of the tripe, Tish?" said Gabe, mischievously.

"Oh, very interesting," I said. "I'd never had tripe before."

"Next time, stick with the filet mignon," Bryan advised. "Right, Belle?" Belle smiled lovingly up at him.

Suddenly I remembered that the presence of Belle undoubtedly meant that Bryan was counting on a good-night kiss. I did not want to kiss Bryan. My conversation began to dry up as my mind started wrestling with this problem. It was left for Bryan and Monica to carry on with the chitchat. I had no idea what they were saying, but finally a voice pierced my consciousness.

"A penny for your thoughts, Tish," said Bryan.

Did he have to keep saying "a penny for your thoughts"? It was going to drive me absolutely bonkers.

"Ten to one," said Gabe, turning the car onto Baker Street, "she's thinking of Miss May and revenge."

"Nah," said Bryan, sounding shocked.

I didn't happen to be thinking of Miss May right that minute, but it had been a good guess. Gabe knew me better than Bryan.

"Creative people often get lost in their thoughts," said Monica kindly. "It's the sign of an original mind, I think."

I began to feel cornered. "I was thinking of lots of things," I said quickly. "Like…uh, cabbages."

"Cabbages?" said Bryan.

"Yep. The price of cabbages has gone up so much lately you might as well eat mushrooms. I ask myself if the days of the common cabbage are behind us and if the cabbage will go the way of the truffle and instead of being something that pigs like to eat will turn out to be a garnish for special occasions so that people end up saying things like 'The wedding reception was lovely, my dear. Lobsters, oysters, and actually cabbages.'"

Bryan and Monica were looking a little confused.

"And then there are the crowned heads of Europe," I went on relentlessly. "There used to be so many kings and queens and now there are hardly any at all. Where are they all now? They're probably all waiting on tables somewhere. I mean, all those distinguished-looking waiters at the Chateau looked like unemployed kings, didn't you think?''

I realized there was a good chance I was convincing everyone present I was nuts, but I was feeling reckless. When I couldn't say what was really on my mind, the only thing I could think to do was to follow the advice of the walrus in *Alice in Wonderland* and talk of cabbages and kings. I didn't see that it mattered what anybody thought of me anyway, at this point.

"I think you ought to give her at least a quarter for those thoughts, Bry," said Gabe, sounding amused. "Well, here's Monica's place."

At first I couldn't figure out why Monica's house looked so familiar. Then I realized it was right next door to Amelia's house. They both were built in the same style—overripe mansion. Monica turned toward us to bid us farewell. "Tish, Bryan, it's been so nice getting to know you," she said. "I hope we'll get to see each other again really soon." She smiled.

I foresaw a great future for Monica in politics. She obviously had more charm than she needed for ordinary social life in Millville.

In the long moments that it took for Gabe to walk her up to her door I found myself wondering if Gabe were succumbing to those beautiful blue eyes, that smile, that sugar and cream voice.

"A penny for your thoughts, Tish," said Bryan softly.

I shall scream, I thought, gritting my teeth. Luckily at that moment Gabe opened the car door and got in. We drove uneventfully on to my house.

When we arrived at my house, Bryan and Belle got out with me to walk me up to the front door. For once, I actually wished Mom and Dad would whip open the front door and ask us in.

"Tish," said Bryan, holding both my hands in his and thus limiting my maneuverability, "this has been such a nice evening for me. But then any evening is nice when I can be with you…down, Belle, for Pete's sake."

Belle had pushed her substantial black snout between us and was pawing at Bryan.

"Heel, Belle," he said sharply. Belle slunk away and he pulled me toward him. I instinctively stepped back, and then it all happened so fast I'm not sure how it happened, but Belle was behind me and I fell over her and landed in Mom's big podocarpus bush. "Eek!" I said. There was a loud clatter as Mom's tin watering can rolled down the walk.

I heard the car door slam and sounds of running within, and suddenly it was like a committee meeting at the doorbell. Mom had flung open the front door, and Gabe was giving me a hand out of the podocarpus bush. "Oh, dear," I said. "I tripped over Belle."

"Are you all right, Tish?" said Bryan, standing stiffly and sounding as if he'd like to do murder, whether to me or Belle I wasn't sure.

"I guess so," I said, brushing myself off. "I didn't realize that Belle was right behind me. Goodness!"

Gabe said, "In football it's a tactic known as the Mickey Mouse tackle." I could tell he was working hard at not smiling.

"I don't think Belle likes me, Bryan," I said in a small voice.

"Don't be silly," said Bryan sharply. "Of course she likes you."

"Well, you'd better come in and get the leaves out of your hair, Tish," said Mom.

I went right in with Mom, but I was pretty sure I heard Bryan saying bitterly as he walked back to the car, "To think I fed you filet mignon, you ungrateful mutt."

Chapter Eight

The next morning in home room I got a note from the office asking me to drop by and see Mr. Morrison after school. Since Westover Academy prided itself on the personal touch with its students, I figured he was just going to ask me how I was getting along now that I was all settled in or something like that. I had such a clear conscience it never even occurred to me to worry about it.

In English class, though, something happened that made me a little uneasy. Miss May asked if anybody could define *persona*. I raised my hand, but she didn't call on me. I looked around and no other hands were raised. That wasn't surprising. *Persona* is not exactly a word that leaps trippingly to the tongue. I wouldn't have known what it meant myself if I hadn't run into it when I was reading up on Dickens. After a minute or so, feeling a little silly, I took my hand down. Miss May went on with the lesson as if I were invisible. It occurred to me that Miss May wished I didn't exist, and she was going to pretend that I didn't. That made me a little nervous. It's no fun having an enemy. Particularly one as mean as Miss May.

The rest of the day the whiskey bottle I had seen in Miss May's room kept weighing on my mind, making me nervous. Could Miss May have guessed somehow that I had found the whiskey bottle? I didn't see how. It was impossible. But when I thought about it, I felt jumpy. If she knew I was in on her little secret, that might explain why she was ignoring me. I didn't like to think what she might do next. An F in class participation might be in the offing.

I was still feeling edgy later that day when I went by Mr. Morrison's office after school, and I peeked cautiously into the office before going in.

"Tish, Tish," he said heartily. "Come in."

I went on in.

"Have a seat! First, let me congratulate you on your really fine cartoon that the *Clarion* printed yesterday." His eyes twinkled. "My wife tells me that it was a good likeness of me. Can't say that I see it myself. I always saw myself as a Cary Grant type instead of the Gerber baby type." He paused a moment, then added uncertainly, "You do know who Cary Grant is, don't you, Tish?"

"Oh, yes, sir."

"Yes, well, the only thing is that we've run into a little problem with that cartoon. Excellent though it was, it did cause some hurt feelings. I'm afraid Miss May was very offended by the depiction of her."

I honestly couldn't understand that because I had deliberately soft-pedaled the picture of Miss May. It was a likeness, but I didn't think you could really say it was an exaggeration.

"I'm sorry to hear that," I said.

"I knew you'd feel that way about it, Tish. I was confident you didn't mean any harm. So why don't you just go by and apologize to Miss May?"

"What?" I said, my voice rising by several decibels. "Did you say apologize to Miss May?"

Mr. Morrison looked at me strangely, and I realized that I was no longer sounding like the well-brought-up young woman my parents had worked so hard to produce. In fact, I was surprised to hear that for an instant I sounded almost like my brother, Blake. I tried to control myself. Polite and calm, I reminded myself. That was the tack to take. "I'm sorry, sir," I said. "But I just can't apologize to Miss May."

"I don't see why, Tish. You told me yourself that you didn't mean any harm. All I want is for you to tell her that."

"I can't."

"But, Tish," he said reasonably, "think of it a minute. If Miss May doesn't have a sense of humor, if she isn't able to laugh at herself, don't you think you should be big enough to apologize and make her feel better? I think her feelings were really hurt."

"Is that what she said?"

"Not exactly. But I can read between the lines."

I could imagine Miss May storming into his office spouting fire and brimstone like a dragon and demanding my apology. Well, she wasn't going to have it. Nobody could make me apologize to her.

"Don't you think you can be big enough to tell her you're sorry?" he said with a winning smile. He did look like the Gerber baby, I decided.

"No," I said. "I haven't done anything to her and I'm not going to say I have."

"You're putting me in a very difficult position, Tish," said Mr. Morrison.

"I expect you're going to expel me," I said resignedly, "or sue me or something like that, but I can't help it. I'm not going to apologize."

I picked up my books and headed toward the door.

"Think it over," Mr. Morrison called as I walked out. "Sleep on it. Talk to your parents about it. You'll feel different tomorrow."

"Ha!" I muttered under my breath.

Talk to my parents about it. That was going to be the catch. Probably as soon as I had left the office Mr. Morrison had picked up the phone to call Dad. This was going to be a war on four fronts. Besides having Mr. Morrison and Miss May after me, I was sure to get lectures from Mom and Dad. But I would never give in. Why should I apologize to Miss May? She was the one who should be apologizing to me! I'd never done anything to her, but she'd been doing her best for weeks to make my life miserable. I could imagine that little half smile that would form on her thin lips if I said I was sorry. I wasn't going to give her the satisfaction. Besides, I *wasn't* sorry. It would be a lie.

"What's up?" said Gabe.

I jumped. "What?" I yelped. I had been so engrossed in my thoughts I hadn't heard him come up behind me.

"I figured something must be up when you walk along muttering to yourself and growling."

I blushed. "I wasn't growling," I said.

"Close enough."

"It's that Miss May," I said finally, lengthening my step in my anger. "She wants me to apologize for the cartoon of her."

Gabe laughed.

"It's not funny," I said irritably. "They'll probably hang me by my thumbs and put my face on Most Wanted posters and throw me out of school and all sorts of things."

"You're not going to apologize?"

"You bet your booties I'm not."

"You'll get a lot of flak."

"Nothing anybody can do will make me change my mind," I said. "Nothing."

"Well, don't grind your teeth at me. I'm not asking you to apologize."

I could imagine the lectures I was going to get from Mom and Dad. I could have written the scripts to them myself. They'd be full of talk about compassion and maturity and looking at things from other people's points of view. Normally I was all for that stuff, but right now I was just mad.

"When is my life going to get easy?" I moaned. "When is it going to be blue skies and lollipops and sugar cookies and lemon drops forever? When do I get a break?"

"Probably never," said Gabe.

"You're right," I said, "because I'm just not that kind of person. I take things too hard."

"I know," he said. "I do, too." And then he grinned.

I immediately felt better. There was something about Gabe that made me feel less ashamed of getting upset. I guess it was because I knew he took things hard, too. Hadn't I heard him say he'd like to pull out Miss May's silly toenails? Hadn't I seen him act like the end of the world had come when Bryan picked up that check at the Chateau? Nobody would call him easygoing. And after all I didn't think he was a horrible person just because he got upset and mad. It made me think that maybe I wasn't so awful either.

Another thing I liked about Gabe was that I could tell him what was on my mind without getting a lecture. My parents were going to be another story entirely.

"My parents are going to be awfully disappointed in me," I said. "And what's more they're going to tell me so over and over again." It was not a cheerful prospect. "They're going to let me know I'm not measuring up to the Summerlin family's high standards."

"What about Blake?" Gabe said. "He'll be on your side."

"Yup," I said glumly, "Blake doesn't measure up either." Lately I had started understanding Blake's point of view for the first time. I had known all along that life was tough for me, but I had only just started realizing, since Gabe had pointed it out to me, that life was tough for Blake, too.

The problem was that Mom and Dad were never going to give up trying to make Blake and me perfect, and unfortunately they had an awful lot of energy and determination. They could be depended on to try it all—lectures, persuasion, psychology, rewards, punishment, more lectures. They weren't the easiest people to live with if, like Blake, you wanted to shlep around bouncing a basketball instead of being a high achiever. And I knew they weren't going to be easy for me to live with when they found out I was refusing to apologize to Miss May.

"Well, would *you* apologize to Miss May?" I said.

"I don't know. It's hard to say. Probably not."

"I can't, that's all. It would be humiliating." I knew Gabe knew about humiliation because I had seen his face that night at the Chateau. "It would be so awful," I went on. "I'm the kind of person who still remembers embarrassing things that happened to me in the second grade. I'll bet if I apologized to Miss May I'd still be thinking about it when I was an old lady. When something happens I really *want* to forget, I just can't forget it. Sometimes I wake up in the middle of the night thinking about embarrassing things that have happened to me."

"I know what you mean," he said sympathetically.

For a second I felt like telling Gabe how much I appreciated his listening to my troubles. I wanted to tell him what a good friend he was. But I knew he wouldn't like it if I did. I was pretty sure now that it was no accident Gabe happened to be around when I was walking home, but there was a sort of unspoken agreement between us to act as if we weren't really friends. I supposed it was because Gabe felt a loyalty to Bryan.

Gabe paused at his driveway. "Well, good luck," he said.

"Onward to the lion's den," I said wearily.

Sure enough, for the rest of the week I got a lot of lectures. Mom and Dad hammered away at me in shifts. I also had to go in and see Mr. Morrison again so he could give me his pitch again about apologizing. And the atmosphere in Miss May's class dropped from frosty to subarctic. So far nobody had threatened to expel me. They all kept trying to appeal to my better nature, instead. As it happened, though, I was so mad at Miss May that my better nature had shrunk to the size of a pea.

As I looked in the mirror it seemed to me that my face had taken on a haunted look, but it never occurred to me to give in. I felt very fatalistic about it. I didn't care what anybody said or did, I knew I wasn't going to apologize.

"I don't know what to say to Stan Morrison," Dad said sorrowfully. "You've always been such a good kid. You've never disappointed us. I can't understand why you're being this way, Tish."

I had already outlined for them in detail Miss May's nastiness to me, so I didn't say anything. I had begun to sense that Mom and Dad were getting resigned to my refusing.

As I turned to go to my room Blake gave me the thumbs up sign. I grinned at him. I was glad I hadn't sold Blake to a passing camel trader or something back when I used to get so annoyed with him, because now I was awfully glad to have him around. At least he was on my side.

I went into my room and closed the door. I was spending a lot of time in there lately. It was the only place I could go and not be lectured. I had been doing a lot of thinking just sitting on my bed in my room. In fact, now that not just Miss May, but Mom, Dad, and Mr. Morrison were all on me, it was amazing how clearly I could think. Lectures in the morning, lectures in the evening, lectures at dinnertime—it was unpleasant, but it concentrated the mind wonderfully.

I began to see that my whole life was neatly divided into things I could do something about and things I couldn't do anything about. For example, I couldn't change the kind of person Miss May was. That was one of the things I couldn't do anything about. But what I could do something about was that I could refuse to apologize to Miss May. Nobody in the world could make me. It gave me a nice warm feeling, like a small glow inside me, to realize that.

Another thing I had realized was that there was no way I could make Gabe ask me out. That was another thing I couldn't do anything about. But the one thing I could do was quit seeing Bryan. Everybody else might think it was great for me to go out with Bryan, but it wasn't making *me* happy. I knew Bryan liked me a lot, and by going out with him again and again I felt as if I were leading him on, making him think I felt the same way about him, when all the time I was only interested in Gabe. It made me feel guilty. I now saw very clearly that I was going to have to break up with him.

While I was brooding on all this suddenly Stephanie burst into my room. "I've got to talk to you, Tish," she said breathlessly. "Your mom said to come straight on back."

"What's wrong?" I said, alarmed.

"It's Spike."

All at once I noticed she had a bandage on her hand. I gasped. "Steph, you don't mean he did that!"

She looked at the bandage. "Not exactly," she said. "You see," she went on quickly, "he kept looking at me and looking at me and I kept getting more and more nervous, wondering, you know, if he was going to get violent, and then this morning he suddenly turned white and asked me to the Christmas dance. I couldn't think *what* to do then," she said, "so I stabbed myself with a dissecting knife."

"You *what*?"

She looked pleased with herself. "Quick thinking, huh? A good thing the biology class left all those things around. I started bleeding all over the place, so Miss Macon sent me to the school nurse to get patched up and the nurse said I should have a tetanus shot and what with one thing and another I never did get back to Biology, thank goodness. So all I need to know is what to say to him when I see him on Monday.''

"I get the idea you don't want to go with him?" I said.

She shuddered. "Tish, he doesn't just look like something that got off a spaceship—he looks like something that crawled out of a black hole.'' She sat down on the bed beside me, her cherubic face looking at me in blind faith. "You're so good at words,'' she said. "I'm counting on you. What do I tell him? Keep in mind that he might get violent.''

I considered the matter broadly and philosophically. It was a question I had been giving an awful lot of thought to myself lately and as far as I could tell it looked very tricky. "It's hard to reject anybody,'' I said, "because you can't reject them without hurting them. Naturally, it's especially hard if the person really seems to like you.''

"Or if you think they might get violent,'' Stephanie piped in.

"How do you tell a boy that you just don't care for him in quite the special way he cares for you?" I said.

"Or that he's totally disgusting,'' put in Stephanie.

"How do you tell him that you like him as a friend but it can never, never be anything more?" I asked.

"Or that you've met sewer rats you liked better,'' said Steph cheerfully.

I sighed. "It's tricky.''

"It certainly is," said Steph. "I was hoping Bobby Harris was going to ask me, but he hasn't yet. The problem is, if I tell Spike I've already got a date he'll ask me who with, so I can't do that. And if I tell him I've decided to go out of town that weekend or that I'm planning to have the flu, then I won't be able to go with Bobby even if he does ask me, because Spike might see us there together."

I stared at the floor. It was perfectly clear that what Steph had to do was say she couldn't go to the dance and then she had to sit home that night no matter who asked her, but I could see why she didn't leap at that idea. Who wanted to sit at home alone when you could be dancing? The problem was that it was easy enough to see what you had to do and it was another thing entirely to do it. For example, I knew I had to break off with Bryan, but I wasn't looking forward a bit to hurting his feelings. In fact, although Stephanie was in a fix with Spike breathing down her neck, I would have traded places with her in a minute.

"I just don't know what to say, Steph," I said miserably. "I just don't know."

Chapter Nine

The next morning, even though it was Saturday, Dad went into the office to catch up on his paperwork and Mom went to a meeting of the Save Our Antique Train Depots committee, so things were momentarily very peaceful at home. Blake was outside in the driveway shooting baskets in the sunshine, and I was curled up under an afghan in the family room reading a book. My book did not have my full concentration, however. I kept thinking about Gabe. He was so clear in my mind that he might have been standing before me in his faded old jeans and banged-up shoes, with the sun picking up the blond streaks in his hair. I knew he spent every Saturday morning at the library. Maybe when Mom got back with the car I could go to the library and accidentally bump into him.

The only thing was, I wasn't sure he would like that. The last time we had seen each other at the library, the time Bryan came in, Gabe had looked as if he wished I would disappear. So maybe I shouldn't go to the library. On the other hand...

I kept arguing back and forth with myself about it. Then the back door slammed and in came Mom, full of good cheer and energy. "Don't you look comfortable all curled up there!" she said. "Don't move, darling. I'm going to fix us some nice hot tea, and we can have a little chat before lunch."

I jumped up, flinging the afghan aside. "Gee, Mom," I said hastily, "I've got to run off to the library." I began scooping up books and papers.

"But it's almost lunchtime," she protested.

"I'll grab a bite uptown," I said. "No time to waste. I've got bunches and bunches of work to do."

I was anxious to get out of there. I knew what "a little chat" meant. It meant another lecture. I had thought Mom was weakening, but apparently sitting around talking about saving train depots with all those other civic-minded ladies had recharged her batteries and now she was all revved up for a talk with me about concern for others, living as a part of a community, and making sacrifices for the common good. With that coming up, I suddenly didn't care whether Gabe wanted to see me at the library or not. I was determined to get out of the house. I grabbed the car keys and charged out the door.

Getting in the car, I glanced at my watch and saw that it was almost noon. If I hoped to run into Gabe, I was cutting it awfully close. He had probably left the library to go out for lunch.

I drove as fast as I dared, but when I got to the library, all the choice parking places out front were already taken. I had to circle the block and park on the other side of the city park that was next to the library. I pulled the car up against the curb and got out quickly.

Suddenly, I saw the last person in the world I wanted to see—Miss May. She was tottering along beside the stream, picking her way along the bank. If we both kept going the way we were going, we would probably collide at the bridge. Why, of all days, did Miss May have to choose today to take it into her head to drink in the beauties of nature at the park?

I hesitated and looked around desperately, thinking I would go the long way around to avoid her. Then, all at once, I heard a splash and realized Miss May had disappeared! I blinked and looked again. She was gone, all right. At first I was so surprised I didn't do anything. Then I broke into a run. I realized she had fallen into the creek. I was going to have to make sure she was okay. I didn't want to, but I didn't see what else I could do. I wasn't sure how deep the water was just there and I didn't even know if she could swim.

I was at the creek's bank in half a minute. I made my way carefully down the bank to the water's edge. "Miss May?" I said. "Are you all right?"

I was relieved to see that the water was only a few inches deep where she had gone in. It would have been easy to wade across it. The only problem was, Miss May wasn't wading. She was just lying there in a few inches of water looking completely zonked out. Her hair had come undone and waved gently in the slowly moving water and her clothes were soaking wet. She seemed to have been knocked out. I wondered if she had hit her head in the fall.

"Miss May?" I said tentatively.

She didn't answer, but wheezed a sound something like "bonk, whiffle." It was proof she was breathing anyway, I thought. I looked at the cold water distastefully, then took off my shoes and long socks and waded in. Yuck. I could feel the mud squishy under my toes, and after the initial shock of cold, my feet began to go numb from the chill. I waded over to her, grabbed her under the arms, and began to tow her to shore. She was a small woman, but since she was a deadweight, it was like dragging a sandbag. Her skirt was trailing in the water and mud as I pulled her along, her hair straggling wet down her neck, and her heels plowing furrows in the muddy bank. She had lost one shoe in the water and the other worked its way off as I dragged her up the bank, exposing her toes, white like her legs and blotchy with the cold. She smelled like the crepes suzette do after Mom splashes the brandy on them, and the smell was so strong I would have been afraid to touch a match to her for fear she would flame up the way the crepes did. It was a relief in a way to smell the brandy because I could be pretty sure, now, that she hadn't bumped her head or hurt herself. Obviously she had just drunk too much.

Somehow I got her up onto the grass. Then I wiped my wet hands on my skirt and tried to catch my breath. I was glad to see that she was breathing fine, because the idea of giving her mouth-to-mouth resuscitation didn't appeal to me a bit. She looked disgusting with her wet hair straggling in her face and her mouth open, sort of snoring. I looked at her despairingly, wondering what I should do next. It was a sunny day, but it wasn't warm, and I was afraid it wouldn't be a good idea just to leave her there until she came to.

Suddenly I heard Gabe's voice. "Good grief!" he yelped.

I looked up in surprise to see him standing on the bridge downstream. He quickly crossed and ran over to us. I had been so intent on getting Miss May out of the water, I'd forgotten all about hoping to run into Gabe. Of course, now I had run into him, but these were not exactly the circumstances I had hoped for. I couldn't think of anything less romantic than the two of us standing over the muddy body of Miss May.

"What happened?" he said, looking shaken. "Is she drowned?"

"Oh, no," I said. "Can't you hear her snoring?"

For all Gabe's coolness when we'd talked about the bottle in Miss May's classroom, I could see he had no more experience with drunks than I did.

"She fell in the stream," I went on. "I just happened to see it, so I fished her out. I think she's drunk."

"Hadn't we better get her to a hospital or something?" he said. "She doesn't look right to me. She's little. I could probably carry her to your car."

I imagined the two of us carrying Miss May's limp body past all the innocent little kids on the sliding board and swings and shuddered. I also imagined what all that mud and dripping water would do to Mom's nice clean car. And what if she got sick on the way or something? What then? Mom might be civic-minded, but I didn't think she was ready to make *that* kind of sacrifice for the common good.

"Maybe we could call the Rescue Squad," I said.

"For a drunk?"

"I can't put her in Mom's car. It would wreck the upholstery. And, after all, for all we know maybe she does need medical treatment. We've got to call the Rescue Squad. The only problem is if we do, there's bound to be an accident report in the newspaper."

"Yeah," said Gabe, looking down at her. "She wouldn't like that a bit."

In Millville you practically couldn't stub your toe without it showing up in the paper. It was probably the horror of that kind of embarrassment that kept Millville's crime rate so low.

"Well, there's no help for it," I sighed. "You stay here with her, and I'll run into the library and call them."

I left Miss May lying on the ground, like a bedraggled, wet kitchen mop, with Gabe standing over her incongruously tall and clean-looking. I dashed over to the library to call the Rescue Squad, then as soon as I got through to them and gave them our location, I went back to the creek to wait for them.

"They're on their way," I told Gabe. The wet hem of my skirt was slapping against my legs and I shivered.

There were some more wheezy sounds from Miss May—bonk, whiffle, boofle. Gabe looked at her unhappily. "Do you think they'll pump out her stomach?" he said.

I plunged my hands into the pockets of my jacket. "I hope they can do something," I said. "It's awful to see somebody in that kind of shape."

"I'll say," he said feelingly.

Soon we heard the siren of the Rescue Squad. They drove the ambulance right up over the sidewalk and onto the grass. Then two men jumped out with a stretcher. They quickly bent over Miss May and began checking her over. A few people had gathered to see what was going on, and I began to feel uncomfortably conspicuous. Then a policeman with a clipboard showed up and started asking questions.

"Do you know if she has taken any pills?" the police officer said.

"We're just innocent bystanders," I said. "We don't know anything."

To my relief the Rescue Squad was losing no time in wheeling Miss May into the ambulance. I knew I was going to feel a lot better now that I didn't have to look at her lying there on the ground.

"You say you didn't see what caused the accident, Miss?" said the police officer.

"Not really," I said. "I just heard a splash, ran over, and dragged her out."

He took my name. "I guess that's it, then," he said, folding the cover of his clipboard closed.

Gabe and I stood there awkwardly for a moment as the ambulance and the police car drove off.

"I don't think I can do any studying after all this," I said. "I'm going to go home. You want a ride?"

He hesitated a minute. "Okay," he said.

We walked across the park toward Mom's car. Gabe had still obviously not recovered from the shock of finding Miss May zonked out and waterlogged. "Boy, it's one thing," he said, "to tell yourself somebody's got a drinking problem, and it's something else to see them like that." He shook his head.

It suddenly swept over me all at once how pathetic she had looked. "Poor Miss May," I said. The whole thing was very unsettling. I suppose I had always figured, without really thinking about it, that grown-ups had things all figured out and under control. To see a teacher flat on her face like that made me feel as if the whole world was less steady somehow. "I feel so sorry for her," I said. "Imagine how embarrassed she's going to be when she comes to and finds out how many people saw her like that. Mom told me that Miss May was probably a pretty unhappy person underneath all that nastiness, and I'm starting to think she was right."

"Does this mean you're going to apologize to her?" Gabe said, looking amused.

"It just means I feel sorry for her, that's all," I said.

"I guess she'll be meaner than ever now," he said. "It's bound to be in the paper, and that's not going to sweeten her disposition any."

"I know. There's one comfort, though. I don't see how she could possibly dislike us more than she does already, so it probably doesn't matter."

We got in the car. Mom's car was an economy model, not the large, Taj Mahal type thing Bryan used. Hers was a small car and in those little bucket seats, Gabe and I were sitting pretty close together. I thought it was kind of nice. I hadn't ever been so close to Gabe before. But it seemed to make him feel uncomfortable, because he abruptly said, "Has Bryan talked to you yet about the Holly Ball?"

I paused with the keys to the ignition in midair. "No," I said, "I'm not going to the Holly Ball with Bryan."

"But he was just saying to me..."

"He hasn't asked me yet, but when he does I'm going to tell him I can't go. I'm not going out with Bryan anymore."

"Hey, you're not still upset about Belle tripping you, are you?"

"Certainly not," I said, starting up the car. "Belle doesn't bother me a bit." This was a flat lie, but I tried to look confident and brave and went on hastily, "It's just that I feel as if Bryan cares more about me than I do about him, and it's making me miserable and I feel guilty and I can't go on like this and so I'm going to stop, that's all." I paused to catch my breath. "Anyway, that's it. I've made up my mind." I put the car in gear and pulled out. We drove in awkward silence for a while.

"Bryan is going to take this hard," Gabe said. "He thinks you're terrific. You should hear him talking about you."

I felt terrible. For the first time I began to feel positively sympathetic to my old boyfriend, Mike, who had so callously dumped me to take up with Mimsy. At the time, I had been so busy feeling sorry for myself that it hadn't occurred to me, but I expect he was feeling like a perfect rat. I could see that now because that's just the way I was feeling about dumping Bryan. I felt like a rat.

"I don't think I want to talk about this anymore," I said. "I wouldn't have said anything, but you seemed to just take it for granted that I was going to the Holly Ball with Bryan, and I'm not."

There was another long silence. Finally I said, "And don't say 'A penny for your thoughts.'"

Gabe laughed, then promptly looked guilty.

"Bryan hardly knows me," I went on, trying hard to make myself feel better. "He may think he likes me, but it's not real. It's just an illusion."

"Well," said Gabe, "he goes on a lot about your perfume, the softness of your touch, the music of your voice."

"Don't," I said.

"Turn here," he said. "This is my street."

I pulled up in front of his house. "I thought it was pretty painful myself," he said. Then he slammed the car door and was gone.

I watched him walking up the driveway toward the house with that distinctive, long-legged stride of his, and I felt a kind of choking sensation. Sometimes I thought I knew Gabe pretty well, but right now I didn't understand him at all. Why did he have to do and make me feel even worse about wanting to break up with Bryan? I had thought we were friends.

I was feeling pretty bleak when I got back to the house. I found Stephanie and Blake in the kitchen sharing a bowl of popcorn. "Where's Mom?" I said, taking off my jacket.

I bent over to blot my wet hem with paper towels, but nobody asked how I had happened to be romping in the water in December, more proof, if I had needed it, that everybody is too wrapped up in their own problems to pay much attention to other people's.

"Mrs. Ellis came by to get her," said Blake. "Friends of the Wildflowers meeting, I think." He stuffed a handful of popcorn in his mouth.

I suddenly realized I hadn't had lunch.

A horn blew outside and Blake jumped up, grabbing his basketball up off a kitchen chair. "Tell Mom I'll be back for dinner," he said, as he charged out the back door.

"Guess what!" said Stephanie the minute he left. I noticed her cheeks were pink with excitement. "I just saw Spike at the grocery store—"

"And his leg was in a cast?" I said, getting a handful of popcorn.

"No, no, but just as good," she said. "You see, I had Mom's grocery list and was at White's, slowly working my way around the store, when suddenly, right at the canned foods, I looked up and there he was! So I told him right out that I couldn't go to the Chrismas dance with him."

I was impressed. "Golly, that was brave of you, Steph."

"Well," she said modestly, "I was holding this big heavy can of peaches, you see. I figured I could always drop it on his toe and run."

"So how did he take it?"

"Pretty well. Once I told him my heart belonged to another, he was very respectful."

"You told him *what*?"

Stephanie looked pleased with herself. "I saw it on an old movie once, so I tried it and it went down pretty well."

"I can't believe you said that."

"Don't argue with success," she said smugly. She promptly stuffed her mouth with popcorn and sat there chewing contentedly like a chipmunk.

The phone rang, and I reached over to the counter absentmindedly and picked it up. "Hello?"

"Tish? This is Bryan."

Suddenly my heart did a somersault. I had decided to break off with Bryan, but unfortunately I hadn't worked out the details yet. I wished I had a little more time to think. What was I going to say?

"Hi, Bry," I said weakly. I desperately hoped he was calling to get an assignment or just to pass the time of day. I looked at Stephanie and suddenly had an idea. "Uh, Bry, I've got company right now. Could I call you back?" I knew I needed time to think.

"This won't take but a minute," he said. "I just wanted to remind you that the Holly Ball is going to be the Saturday after Christmas. So mark it on your calendar, okay?"

I felt my grip on the phone weakening. He seemed to take it so much for granted that we were going together that if I hadn't already told Gabe I was going to break off with Bryan, I think I would have backed out, but now I knew I had to go on with it. I couldn't risk Bryan's hearing from Gabe that I planned to break off with him before I had told him so myself.

"Uh, I can't go, Bryan," I said.

"Huh? Why not?"

I looked desperately around the room as if expecting a cue card to fall down from the ceiling. "Uh...uh..."

"Are you okay, Tish?" Bryan said. "Can you hear me all right? I said what's up?"

My whole life flashed before my eyes. "Because my heart belongs to another," I croaked.

There was dead silence at the other end. Then Bryan said, "Oh, I see," in a hurt voice. "Then this is goodbye, I guess."

I hung onto the phone a few seconds listening numbly to the dial tone, then I slammed the receiver down. "I can't believe I said that!" I wailed. "I can't believe it. It's all your fault, Stephanie. My mind was such a blank, that awful line of yours just floated up in it." I ran my fingers through my hair frantically. "Ooh, how humiliating. What if he tells somebody what I said? What if he tells *Gabe* what I said? I'll die. He'll think I'm crazy to go around talking like some dumb old movie." I threw myself heavily into a chair. "I need an aspirin," I groaned. "I am having the most horrible, terrible, awful, unspeakable day."

"What you said worked, didn't it?" Stephanie said calmly, taking another handful of popcorn. "Honestly, Tish. You take things too hard. You know, what we need is something to drink. Got any root beer?"

Chapter Ten

After that horrible, terrible, awful, unspeakable day I tried to pick up the pieces of my life and go on. I worked at looking on the bright side. It was true that my life was a mess in every concrete way, but on the other hand maybe I had made certain indefinable spiritual advances. I didn't hate Miss May anymore, for example. That should count for something. I still basically couldn't stand her, but I also felt sorry for her. She was actually kind of pathetic.

I was getting resigned to my life being a mess, too. I wasn't sure whether that was a spiritual advance or not, but since I was trying to cheer myself up I decided I might as well count it as one. My biggest fear was that Bryan would tell Gabe what I had said to him on the phone, but it didn't seem as if there was much I could do about that one way or another, so I tried to be philosophical about it.

Monday, when I got to English class, I avoided looking at Miss May. The Sunday newspaper had reported that she fell in the creek, but they hadn't given any details. I was hoping nobody would mention it, but just as class was starting, Eliot piped up and asked her about it. You had to wonder how bright he was.

"Thank you for your concern, Eliot," she said coldly, "but I am fine. Since I had influenza I have unfortunately been subject to fainting spells, but in this case, luckily, no harm was done. I am feeling much better now."

She shot me a steely look that dared me to contradict her. I shrank back into my seat and breathed shallowly for some minutes, but we went on with the lesson for the day with no further problems. As soon as class was over, I threw pride to the winds and more or less ran out of there.

I wanted to get away from Miss May, but most of all I wanted to avoid running into Gabe. If Bryan had told him what I said on the phone, I was going to die of embarrassment. I was trying so hard to avoid him that not only did I run out of Miss May's class, but later, after school, I made sure I was out in front of the school in plenty of time so I could be certain of catching my ride home with Blake. Unfortunately, this had to be the day Blake forgot all about me.

With dismay I watched Mom's car zip out from the direction of the school parking lot and go careening down Oak Street while I stood at the circular drive completely ignored.

"Missed your ride again?" said Gabe's voice behind me. I wheeled around to face him, feeling myself go hot from head to toe.

"I think I've slipped Blake's mind," I said. For once it didn't cheer me up to see Gabe. When I thought about what I had said to Bryan on the phone I wished I could disappear into the cement. I wondered if I dared to hope that he hadn't repeated it to Gabe.

As we started walking home in silence, I kept looking at the ground a lot, wishing I was someplace far away.

"I was talking to Bryan last night," Gabe said finally.

I swallowed hard.

"I told him I had put in my application at Hamburger Heaven for an after-school job," Gabe went on.

I forgot my embarrassment and looked at him open-mouthed. "You mean you aren't going to be Bryan's reader anymore?" I said.

"Nope," he said. "And the funniest thing was, when I told him he got mad and asked me if I was the other man in your life! What do you figure he meant by that?"

I choked a little, but I finally managed to say in a small voice, "I think when people are upset, what they say doesn't always make sense."

"I guess that's it," he said. There was another silence, then he said, "So I get the idea you and Bryan have broken up."

"That's right." I didn't trust myself to say more.

"Then maybe you'd like to go to the Holly Ball with me," he said diffidently. "Unless you're already going with somebody else or something."

"Oh, no," I said. "I mean, yes! I mean, I'd love to go with you." I could feel myself blushing again.

Gabe looked uncomfortable, too. "I don't have a fancy car like Bryan," he said.

I looked at him in surprise. Surely Gabe didn't imagine that girls liked to go out with him only because he was driving that fancy car of Bryan's!

"Good grief, Gabe," I said. "Nobody cares what kind of car you drive."

"I know how girls like to get dressed up and go to fancy places," he said.

"I think girls just like to spend time with people they like, that's what I think," I said.

"I'll be driving my dad's 1975 Plymouth with the rusted chassis," he said with studied casualness.

I stomped my foot in exasperation. "I *want* to go to the Holly Ball with you," I said. "I don't care if you pick me up on a bicycle."

He laughed and suddenly I got a glimpse of the old knock-em-dead, arrogant Gabe I remembered so well. "I guess I'm a little bit weird on the subject of money," he admitted.

I was feeling a pleasant warm glow all over. Gabe actually liked me. He had even quit his job with Bryan so he would feel free to ask me out. He was actually willing for Bryan to be mad at him and only for the pleasure of my company. For once, my life was going along the way it would have if I had written the script myself.

He slipped his arm around my waist and we walked on that way awhile. My feet scarcely seemed to touch the ground. It seemed no time until we got to his house. "Here's my stop," he said.

As he turned to leave I smiled in his direction. I tried to make it a nice middle-of-the-road sort of smile, neither soppy and gooey like melted cheese nor vampy and glamorous like in the movies. It was tricky, and I decided I had better practice at the mirror when I got home.

He smiled back and I felt faint with happiness. "Okay, then," he said, "see you tomorrow."

I floated the rest of the way home. I was so high that if I'd had an aerosol can of smoke I could have done sky-writing. I would have written "Gabe likes me." That was certainly news that deserved to be written in the sky or spelled out in lights or possibly embroidered on a T-shirt with hearts and flowers. However, I settled for merely calling Stephanie when I got home and telling her.

"Gabe has asked me out!" I said, when I reached her. "He *likes* me."

"Gabe," she said thoughtfully. "Now, is he the blind guy?"

"No!"

"Don't tell me! Now I remember. Is he the one you did the caricature of in class that day?"

"Steph, you have not been paying attention," I said severely. "Gabe is the one I have been hoping would ask me out."

"Oh. Well, that's good."

It was not as satisfying as spelling the news out in lights, but given the circumstances of my life, it was going to have to do.

As I hung up I gave a passing thought to the notion that I should never have left Senior High. Stephanie had never had any trouble keeping the cast of characters of my life straight when we went to the same school and knew the same people. If I had stayed on at Senior High, the pain of seeing Mike and Mimsy together would have dulled in time. Also, if I had stayed I could have completely missed being at war with Miss May. Of course, I had to remember that I would probably have never gotten to know Gabe either. Probably it was a fair trade-off.

The night of the Holly Ball turned out to be easily the happiest night of my life so far. For Christmas I had asked for a special dress for the ball, and Mom came through with a zinger she had made herself. There are times when I am actually grateful for all her energy and determination, and the nights she was sitting up late slaving over those taffeta ruffles were among those times. The dress she made was sophisticated without being daring, striking without being conspicuous, and gorgeous without driving us bankrupt. "It's perfect," I breathed, as Mom zipped me into it.

"Come on in here and let me see it," Dad called to me.

I skipped into the family room.

"Pretty, very pretty," he said. "Now don't go dashing out of here so fast we don't get to have a little chat with your young man."

"It's Gabe, Dad. You've already had a little chat with him."

"Gabe?" said Dad, looking blank.

Mom adjusted a ruffle to get it to lie flat. Her mouth was still full of pins from the last-minute adjustment she'd had to make to the hem, and she took them out so she could speak. "Bryan's friend," she said. "You remember him—the future soldier of fortune."

"Whatever happened to Bryan?" Dad said. "He was such a good kid."

"He did seem like a nice boy," sighed Mom.

"He was not for me," I said, twirling around to make the shirt flare out in a bell shape. It was going to be fun dancing in this dress. "Besides," I went on, "the relationship had no future. His dog couldn't stand me. You wouldn't want your daughter to be gobbled up by a Labrador retriever, would you?"

"I have more realistic worries," said Mom dryly. "Are you sure this Gabe person is a nice boy?"

"Gabe is absolutely the most fascinating boy I've ever met."

Just then the doorbell rang and I made a dash for it, leaving Mom saying, "I didn't ask if he were fascinating, Tish. I asked if he were *nice*."

When I flung the door open, there was Gabe, stamping his feet to keep warm, his breath frosty in the night air, his hair neatly combed. I thought he looked great, and when he saw me and broke out his magic smile, I think the effect may have been felt even by Mom, standing back in the foyer, because all she said as we dashed off for the car was, "Have a good time!"

There was a full moon, and I did not notice any rust on the car as Gabe opened the door for me. It seemed like Cinderella's coach to me. Inside, the upholstery was split in places and there was the familiar homey smell of a family car that has been used for years to haul everything from fertilizer for the garden to sticky ice cream. I slid in feeling delightfully happy.

As Gabe turned the key and the motor leapt to life, he said over the roar of the engine, "I talked to Bryan this morning and he wants me to come back and work as his reader again."

I could feel a little of the bloom of my happiness wearing off at the mention of Bryan's name.

"I was glad," he said simply. "I liked the job better than frying hamburgers, and it's the sort of thing I can combine with my own studying. Besides, I've been kind of missing old Bryan."

It occurred to me that Bryan's offering Gabe his job back must mean he wasn't mad anymore. "That's great!" I said enthusiastically. "That just goes to show that Bryan was never that keen on me, don't you think? It's terrific that he's not mad. We can all be friends now."

I saw the white flash of Gabe's teeth in the dark as he grinned. "Well, he did say he thought we'd forget about ever double-dating," he said.

"Oh."

"I'll bet I know what you're thinking," Gabe said. "You're thinking, why can't life be simple. Why do there always have to be these rotten complications."

"I was sort of thinking that," I admitted. "How did you guess?"

"I think it all the time myself," he said.

The Holly Ball was at the country club. The academy was renting their ballroom for the occasion. The front door was banked on either side, as we went in, with rows and rows of potted poinsettias. There were an awful lot of poinsettias there, and as I walked past them I felt a little nervous. I had never been inside a country club before, and I was a little worried I would feel intimidated by all the grandeur. I had already decided after that dinner at the Chateau that I wasn't cut out for grandeur. When we got inside, though, and found the ballroom, it turned out that it wasn't all that different from our church's basement recreation hall, and I felt right at home. I had to admit it was prettier than the church basement, though, with fairy lights strung across the ceiling like stars, a wall of mirror, and lots of big, stiff, gold lamé bows as decorations. The dance floor was already packed with kids and the band was playing at full blare. Gabe and I found a patch of floor to dance on and pretty soon the music switched to dreamy. Christie and Eliot danced past us. I was glad to see that Christie looked as if she were having a good time.

"Hey, Gabe," said Eliot. "Did you hear about Miss May?"

Gabe promptly pulled me over closer to Eliot and Christie, the better to hear the latest news.

"No, what?" he said. "Tell us."

"The cops caught her weaving down Somerset Avenue yesterday."

"You're kidding me!" Gabe said.

The four of us gave up all pretense of dancing and stood there in the middle of the ballroom talking about Miss May.

"That's right," said Eliot. "They charged her with DUI and let her make one phone call to her lawyer, that's what I heard."

"Boy, she's going to need a lawyer," I said, appalled. Driving under the influence is a really serious offense in North Carolina.

"Maybe they'll put her in jail for a long time," said Eliot with relish. And even sweet Christie looked pleased.

I was glad I had passed the point of really hating Miss May, because Eliot looked pretty unpleasant standing there obviously panting for Miss May's blood.

"But that's not the best part," said El. "My dad's on the academy's board of directors, and he says Miss May has handed in her resignation. She's going to go into an alcohol rehabilitation program."

"Oh, good!" I said. "Maybe they can fix her up."

Everybody looked at me as if I were nuts.

"I don't know what you mean by 'fix her up,'" Gabe said, "but I don't think they give them head transplants at that kind of place."

"I just feel sorry for her," I said, feeling a little squirmy as everyone looked at me incredulously.

"But just think, Tish," Christie said earnestly, "they'll have to bring in a teacher now who is a real human being, somebody maybe even who's nice and has a sense of humor."

I had to admit it sounded good.

"I think this calls for a celebration," said Gabe. "Come on, Tish. Let's hit the punch bowl."

We were warm even though we hadn't been dancing long. There were a lot of people in that room.

Gabe and I made our way over to the punch bowl and got a couple of cups of punch. He looked at his thoughtfully, the red punch gleaming like a jewel in its clear plastic cup. "I was going to say, 'Let's toast to revenge,'" he said, "but now I have a better idea. Let's toast to forgiveness."

"That sounds good to me," I said. I knew what was on Gabe's mind. It wasn't just Miss May he was thinking about, but Bryan. He was remembering how we had hurt him. For that matter, I had a private thought, too. I was remembering how awful I had felt when Mike had dumped me for Mimsy. It didn't bother me to think about it now, because I could see that Stephanie had been right when she said Mike's dumping me didn't mean that I was a rotten person. It was just that Mike and Mimsy had clicked the way Gabe and I clicked. But I sure had been miserable there for a while.

Miss May had done her bit to make me miserable, too, if it came to that. And unlike Mike she had done it on purpose. But to be fair about it, probably I had hurt her, too. If she hated the way she looked, it must have been awful to pick up the school paper and find herself in that cartoon of mine right on the front page.

When I thought about it, the whole world seemed to be such a circle of hurting and getting hurt every which way you looked that I couldn't think of a better thing to toast than forgiveness, and I raised my glass silently to Gabe's.

"Golly, it's hot in here," Gabe said suddenly, looking around.

"It's because the place is full of people," I said.

He put down the cup of punch and took my hand. "Let's go outside."

He led me across the crowded dance floor to some tall curtained doors on the other side of the room, and we stepped out of them to find ourselves on a kind of cement-floored balcony with an iron railing.

It was freezing cold out there, but it certainly was pretty. The full moon cast a pallid glow over the tennis courts and the rolling grass of the distant golf course. Closer to us, the moonlight danced in a hundred splintered lights on the swimming pool.

Gabe didn't seem to notice that I was shivering. "Tish," he said, a worried crease appearing over his dark eyebrows, "you know when I said I didn't go out with the same girl two times in a row?"

"Yep," I said, stamping my silver slippers to keep warm.

"I think I'm changing my policy," he said.

I smiled and blew warm breath on my fingers to keep them from freezing. "That's nice," I said, my teeth chattering.

"The thing is, I think it would be nice if we got to know each other better," he said. "What do you think?"

I could tell that Gabe was getting really nervous about possibly going out with the same girl two times in a row. He looked as if he were about to jump off the balcony into the icy swimming pool.

"Let's go inside where it's warm," I managed to say in spite of my chattering teeth.

He opened the door, and I scooted inside quick as a rabbit. "I thought girls went for balconies," he said, a little puzzled.

"Girls go for warm ears," I said, breathing the heated air of the ballroom with relief, "and warm feet and warm hands and so forth."

"I guess you're not the romantic type, are you?" he said.

"I guess not. Maybe I'm more the down-to-earth, everyday kind of person."

He looked relieved. "That's good," he said. He put his arm around me and we started dancing. The tiny fairy lights whirled and swirled above us, and I realized that in just a few days a brand new year would be beginning. Somehow, I felt absolutely certain that this one was going to be a good year, a blue skies and lollipops and sugar cookies and lemon drops forever kind of year, because I knew I was absolutely going to love Gabe and me getting to know each other better.

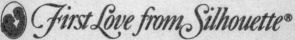

First Love from Silhouette

DON'T MISS THESE FOUR TITLES— AVAILABLE THIS MONTH . . .

BLUE SKIES AND LOLLIPOPS
Janice Harrell
When Tish changed schools to avoid a sticky romantic situation, she found she had only jumped from the frying pan to brave the fire.

AND MILES TO GO
Beverly Sommers
From the moment Tom first saw Sandy, she began to run through his mind. Would they ever be on the same track?

BLOSSOM INTO LOVE
Mary Jean Lutz
Latina's plans for a fun social summer had gone awry. This turned out to be a blessing in disguise, especially when she got to know Tully.

BIRDS OF PASSAGE
Miriam Morton
Tavia had a chance to live out her fantasies when she took a glamorous holiday cruise. But would Hall fly away once their ship came home?

WATCH FOR THESE TITLES FROM FIRST LOVE COMING NEXT MONTH

ORINOCO ADVENTURE
Elaine Harper
A Blossom Valley Romantic Adventure!
When Juanita heard charismatic Tom Goulding describe the Community Health program, she was determined to join the group—even if it meant traveling to the wilds of Venezuela.

VIDEO FEVER
Kathleen Garvey
Who would have guessed that when arch enemies Nell and Daniel were forced to collaborate on a video project they would zoom in and focus on their very personal script?

THE NEW MAN
Carrie Lewis
In spite of himself, when Rick Masterson decided to compete for the Young Miss Homemaker Award, he became the model for the liberated man. Heidi was not surprised. She had known the real Rick all along.

WRITE ON!
Dorothy Francis
Vonnie was on the move again! The heroine of *Special Girl* and *Bid for Romance* had attendant problems to solve: just who was sending her those threatening notes, and why?

First Love from Silhouette